CARGON
HONOUR & PRIVILEGE

KIMBERLY GOULD

WWW.MARTINSISTERSPUBLISHING.COM

Published by

SkyVine Books, a division of Martin Sisters Publishing, LLC

www.martinsisterspublishing.com

ISBN: 978-1-937273-00-2

Science Fiction/Fantasy

Printed in the United States of America

Martin Sisters Publishing, LLC

DEDICATION

Thank you to Ruth Perkins and Sharyn McCart
for their help in bringing Eve to Life.

~

Dedicated to Delilah and Allen,
for bringing me to life.

SKY VINE BOOKS

Science Fiction/Fantasy

An imprint of Martin Sisters Publishing, LLC

CHAPTER ONE

"Eve, attend." The Headman pulled Eve's attention from her classmates. "You will observe wine service tonight. Tomorrow, this will be your assignment."

"Yes, sir," Eve answered quietly, bobbing a very small and quick curtsy, appropriate for such a high servant. She ran to Sarah, her brown skirts kicking around her. "I've been given a new assignment, wine service!" she told her red-haired friend. Eve swept strands of hair away from her eyes.

"I'm so happy for you!" Sarah gushed. "You have to run and tell your parents. I will tell the others. I hope I get wine service, too, one day. Do you think I might?" Sarah smoothed her dress and hair.

Eve pecked her cheek. "I'm sure you will. You just need to be a little steadier with your dishes. The Wine Master won't accept a Server who slops!" Eve teased.

Sarah laughed. "I would hope not. How terrible." Such incidents were not unheard of, but Servers unable to complete their tasks cleanly were usually reassigned very quickly. There were easily four or five servants for every elite member, although most did not have a single dedicated Server. Only the Most High were able to claim such luxury. The others shared personal Servers within their families.

The elite preferred the most beautiful servants for dinner and personal service. “Well, go on! You will need to hurry.”

After visiting both her parents and the hair dresser, Eve entered the kitchen, now nearly empty of kitchen staff, with only a few tending fires to keep the food warm, and found the Wine Master. “Yes? Ah, the new Server, of course. Your name?” he asked.

“Eve.”

“Yes, excellent. Please attend Lane. He will show you your duties for tomorrow night.” The Wine Master indicated a young man with black hair and fair skin.

“Lane?” she asked to be sure she had the right Server. He nodded to her. She took note of his dark, almost black eyes. “I am Eve. I shall attend you tonight.”

“Ah, a new Server. This is the red. This, the white.” He held both pitchers down so that she might see and smell them. “They are difficult to confuse. Most elite will only have one all night, but others choose the one best matching the course being served. You will get the idea.” He stepped out to a space between two long tables. Eve watched from a place against the wall as Lane moved from one elite to another checking their cups. He never stopped moving up and down the tables although on most passes he poured nothing.

Over the course of the evening, Eve noticed the three-tiered board at the end of the hall. While scurrying with empty dishes, it had never caught her attention. She only glanced at it now between instructions from Lane. There were thirteen pieces on it, and they seemed to be all different shapes. She had no idea why it was given such a prominent place in the hall, opposite the High Table.

In the dorm, after dinner, she released her hair and replaced her comb. Sarah was already on her mattress, but her other roommates were waiting so they could each hug her and offer congratulations.

Eve spent the morning mopping the hall with the other Servers and Platters. From the corner of her eye, she watched the other Servers polishing. She tried to observe the technique so she would be ready when it was her turn at this chore. She also got a closer look at the three-tiered board as she mopped under its table. The table it perched on was easily as ornate as the High Table, inlaid with pictures of the thirteen pieces.

That night she was placed to serve between two tables. One held Princes and Princesses, the other Ducat and Ducati. Her tables were between those of two male Servers. One was Lane, and the other was Denis. Denis whispered his name to her when they each reached the ends their adjoining tables. They helped her through the meal; she was able to lift a pitcher while looking at Lane or Denis at the beginning of a course to be sure she knew which was the correct wine.

At the end of dinner, Denis came and clapped her on the shoulder. “Great service; very efficient. You will be an excellent Server.”

Eve flushed at the compliment and smiled at him. “Eve,” she said as she hadn’t given her name earlier.

“A pleasure to meet you, Eve. You will make a fine replacement for Donna.”

“Where is she serving now?” Eve asked, not knowing why there was an opening at dinner service.

“Oh,” Lane looked around to make sure no one was close. “She developed acne. She is serving among the wardrobe until her complexion clears or another duty is offered her.”

Acne? Eve only barely knew what that was. A blemishing of the skin. Of course, if Donna’s appearance was compromised, the elite would want her to serve elsewhere. Only the loveliest served at dinner service, which was why her parents had been so happy for her when she started running dishes. Eve prayed that Donna be given a duty which she enjoyed, whether that be returning to dinner service or not.

Wardrobe sounded like a fine duty. Eve knew nothing about stitching, but the concept seemed soothing; fastening pieces of cloth together, pressing, cleaning, folding. If the acne was not too bad, Donna might be chosen by one of the Highnesses and serve as a personal servant for their family. Donna would find a place for herself in time, Eve was certain. If she was like Eve, she found joy in doing her best in whatever duty she was given.

Even when simply shuttling plates, Eve had been happy to be able to help the elite have their dinner more smoothly, facilitate conversations that would decide the fate of Fontive and give them reprieve from the responsibilities they faced during the day. She had heard of some servants who were unsatisfied in their lot, who sought easier duties or higher stations. Most were never satisfied and ended up punished or exiled to farms. She had never been one of these. Her parents had each found duties which suited their temperaments and talents, and so Eve was certain she would as well. She was uncertain now just what such a duty would be. She was happy with wine service for the moment, but she would of course outgrow this duty, as she had the one before. Dinner was not a long-lived service. As servants aged, they were moved from the hall into other duties. Eve would like to teach the servant children, as Elsa did, but of course there was only one instructor, so this duty was unlikely to be open to her.

She visited with Lane and Denis, while polishing the service sets the next day. The small rag and metallic smelling compound suited her meticulous nature. She reviewed the wine and food combinations she had learned so far, listed the titles of the elite from High One to Ernst. She reviewed the titles in her second language, and named the pieces of the service in that language as well. Lane and Denis had both been attending dinner for two years. They introduced her to others, corrected any mistakes she made, and generally helped her through her first full day.

They also accompanied Eve when she joined her roommates in the garden during their free time. Denis took an instant liking to Sarah, and Eve hoped more than ever that her friend be moved into wine service in future.

She had been serving wine for two months when a Prince rose from one of her tables to challenge one from another table. Both were older men, older than her father. They each took their wine and moved to the board with thirteen pieces. She saw her Prince raise one piece from the board and move it. She checked two more cups and looked up to see his opponent had also made a move. She noted these two pieces moved in different patterns. When she had finished her pass of the table, she stepped forward to the carved table and refilled her Prince's cup.

"No more," he told her after the refill, and she did not approach again. Through the rest of dinner, she took the time she could to examine the boards. The pieces were arrayed around a place in the center of the middle board. It seemed clear that this was the goal and the pieces were all trying to take it. She kept this in mind as she tended to her tables. She continued to watch the game, learning each piece's range, his tactic, his defence.

The game ran for many hours. Several elite would rise, watch the board for a time, and then leave. Soon only a few elderly Princes and Princesses, as well as the High One, were left. Eve nodded to her fellow Servers, cocking her head. The wine master had refilled both her pitchers; she could serve all that were left until the end of the match. She moved among the observers, filling cups as she passed. The game ended when her Prince placed a piece on the goal. There was applause from the observers, and the loser unpinned a medal from his robe and gave it to the winner. Eve had no idea what this signified. Her Prince pinned it to his chest, and they began to put the pieces into their starting positions. She stepped around the observers to offer a last cup to the Princes. They each took one and toasted one another.

Eve took her pitchers back to the wine master as the final members of the elite filed out. Rather than head to her dorm, Eve stepped back through the door from the kitchen and stood behind the High Table. The High One had not left either. Eve wondered why She lingered. The High One carefully lifted a piece, swept a scrap of silk over the man and his place on the board, then replaced him. Eve had not seen any of the servants attend the board in her two months of dinner service. She would never have guessed the High One Herself saw to this task. After two pieces she called Eve forward.

"Come, child. You are curious." Her voice was strong, full of her authority. The High One was of middle age, only slightly older than Eve's own mother. Her face had fine lines at the corners of her eyes and lips. Her hair was piled in elaborate whorls over her head and threaded with tiny jewels. Her robe was an exquisite, regal purple and lined with fur. Her gown glittered with metallic threads. The scrap was simple undyed silk. It was a sharp contrast.

Eve stepped forward, head bowed deeply.

"Look up. You cannot see from down there." The High One did not touch Eve, but it felt as if fingers had been placed beneath her chin. She watched the High One lift a third piece and give it the same careful treatment. "Cargon," she intoned replacing the piece. "You must never touch this board. Never touch a piece upon it."

Eve did not dare to speak, neither nodding nor shaking her head, but her eyes widened. She would never suppose to take any action that was not wished of her.

The High One's face softened. "You saw your first match, didn't you? That is always when the interest is piqued. Tell me, child, did you understand the game?"

"Yes, Most High." She felt ashamed and blushed as soon as she spoke the words. To assume she could have learned such an elite thing in such a short time was brazen in the extreme.

The High One merely smiled and Eve felt she had been granted the greatest of honours. "Then you are bright. Perhaps someone will initiate another match while you watch. Perhaps I shall see to it your brightness is not wasted." The High One turned from Eve then to continue her work.

Eve desperately wanted to ask why the High One performed this task. Surely someone else could and should perform this service. When the duty was done Eve still stood, head bowed, as the High One departed. Then she returned to her room. She uncoiled her hair and undressed in the dark; the others had long since turned in for the night. The next day she did not tell any of her fellow Servers about her encounter with the High One although many discussed the match.

"I saw a Ducat lose his wife at the board," one older girl told them. "It was in my third month of service, three years ago." Spouses could be traded on the outcome of a game? Eve was appalled.

"Eve, how did the match last night end?" Denis asked

"The Prince from my table won. He was given a medal from the chest of the other. Then they toasted with the last of the wine."

"That's remarkably more sedate than the last one. The loser had to back out of the hall from shame," another Server chimed in.

That night, Eve lingered after dinner again. She saw the High One, alone, tending to the board and its pieces that night, and the night after, and the night after that. She always completed the task in the same order, the same manner. It was a ritual. The High One never called Eve forward again.

Two weeks after seeing her first Cargon match, the Headman called on Eve as she arrived at the hall in the morning. "Eve, your morning duties are being reassigned. Follow me." Her eyes went wide, and she looked to her friends among the Servers. Sarah had been called to wine service just the day before; Eve hadn't even gotten to greet her yet this morning.

"Yes, sir," she said, following. Her friends' eyes were sympathetic. They, like Eve, thought this meant she was no longer on dinner service. As she followed, Eve tried to determine what her fault had been. Certainly not her attention to her duties; she had performed flawlessly both during dinner and in the mornings. She was no less pretty than she had been when called to wine service. Was it because she tended to linger in the hall? Was it not permitted? No one had told her so.

The Headman paused at a pair of polished wooden doors. "This is the library. You have been granted access to its contents. Mind the Librarians when you are within." Eve bowed her head, even more confused. She had access to the library, but she was not to be a Librarian? Those were the servants of the library, of course. They ranked only just below the Headman himself. She would be honoured to serve with them.

The Headman turned from the doors and led her through more halls. She was in the elite portion of the palace. Eve had never been down these corridors. She took care to remember her route. The walls were now lined with paintings and tapestries instead of simple patterns. The floors were polished tiles instead of wooden planks. She was glad she wore her slippers rather than hard-soled shoes. The doors were no longer simply wooden, but inlaid with metal and enamelled. He brought her to one with a tree depicted on it.

"You are to attend here every morning until the noon bell. Your afternoons are still your own, and you shall attend dinner service as before." He nodded briefly and left her.

She mumbled, "Yes, sir," but he was already striding back they way they had come. She opened the door carefully and peeped inside. The room was empty, but she heard people coming down the hall. She quickly ducked in, closing the door behind her. She went to the far wall and stood, awaiting instructions. Surely another servant would find her here soon. She was shocked when not a servant but an Ernst entered — an Honoured elite, the lowest of them. The woman looked to her at the back of the room, and Eve bowed her head. The Ernst moved books and pages on the table at the front. Looking from under her lashes, Eve saw the Ernst was a little younger than her parents, a woman with a presence that exceeded her station. She was broad at shoulder and hips. Her chestnut hair fell over her shoulders in a multitude of braids.

While she waited for instructions, more elite entered, these of all ranks. Their clothes were a myriad of colours and styles as suited their families. Boys and girls, they ranged in age from six years to nine. They took seats on the benches throughout the room, facing the Ernst. Eve desperately hoped she was still in the right position, ready to serve. Who would give her instruction? None of these, certainly.

One girl came to stand before her, a Ducati child. Eve curtsied. The girl could not have been much more than six. She was dressed in a deep red robe embroidered in blue over a yellow under dress. Her hair was as light as Eve's and braided simply down her back. She had freckles on her nose. She bent a little twisting her neck to look up at Eve.

"Highness Josephine, would you please take a seat?" the Ernst requested to Eve's relief. "You will find today's lesson most informative, I think. It relates to proper conduct toward servants." Her voice was slightly amused and several of the Ducati's classmates chuckled quietly. The girl's face flushed crimson, and she quickly took a seat next to a boy in a red coat – probably a relative.

The Ernst began to lecture, "Some of you may not be aware, but the serving class have a rank system not unlike our own. It is not necessary for you to know all of its intricacies, but today, I will share with you those ranks with which it is acceptable for us to interact." Eve brought her head up. She was afraid of offending the Ernst, but found it easier to focus on her words when looking to her lips.

Throughout the lesson, most of which Eve was familiar with, the Ernst looked to elite in the benches, but her eyes never came to Eve. This made her feel more comfortable in looking up. The children learned the various divisions of servants which fell under the Masters. They also learned the ranking of the Masters, beginning with the Master Librarian and ending with the Grounds Master, to whom Eve's father reported. She learned that it was unacceptable for elite to touch most servants except to bestow an honour, for above excellent service.

She knew how demeaning it was for a servant to touch an elite. She had been drilled in such things when she was younger than even that Ducati who had approached her, but she never knew that her safety from abusive elite was equally assured by the shame they would receive from touching her. Indeed several examples of elite exiled, or demoted from the elite entirely, were offered to the class. All were from times before Eve was born.

The young elite were also instructed on the loss of honour incurred by a servant for looking into the eyes of an elite without permission. The Ernst singled out the Ducati once more, to explain the types of demotion and duty that might be assigned to a servant who was unfortunate enough to be in breach of this custom. The Ducati blushed again and slunk a little on her bench.

Finally, the Ernst distributed pages to all the children and asked each to fill in the positions of the Masters and which was most likely to be in contact with their parents in their duties. The children, pages in hand, rose and began to file out. Just as the last were reaching the door, Eve heard the noon bell. She had ducked her head as the children rose, but now lifted it slightly to see who remained. Only the Ernst was still in the room, and she was picking up her last book. Eve waited for her to drift through the door and then followed behind, closing the door behind her.

After a very quick noon meal, in which Eve avoided her friends for the most part, she headed for the library. She had no idea what to tell her friends about her new duty. It wasn't really a duty at all; she wasn't providing a service in her new position, unless it was as an example for the class. She did wave though, briefly, with a smile. Hoping they would understand that she was well, she would try to think of something to tell them before dinner service.

She opened one of the library doors and was approached by a Librarian. The man wore spectacles! She had never seen such things outside the elite. She tried not to stare and cast her eyes past him to the shelf behind, lined with books.

"Ah, yes," he muttered, not really addressing her. "Put things back as you found them, obviously," he muttered again, now paging through a book in his hands. He continued on his path to another part of the library.

Unsure what to do, she decided to explore first. On either side of the door were two long tables with books scattered across them. Now she saw other Librarians moving the books into piles on those tables and taking handfuls with them around the room. She followed one and watched as she placed the books back on various shelves. From those shelves, Eve moved to another part of the room, a large circular open area with tables and chairs around the edges. The shelves began again behind these. Those elite in the library seemed to be here. Occasionally one would call a Librarian and request a book. She saw tall windows behind one section of the circular area and moved to look out into the garden. Her friends were playing in the green. She smiled and turned back to the room. The knowledge here called to her. She had gratefully devoured every book on her small schoolroom shelf. Here there were so many more.

She wandered many of the aisles, reading titles from spines. She quickly discerned the sorting system. Finding a section on etiquette, she decided to start there, as this was what her class seemed to be studying. Rather than servant-elite or even elite-servant protocols, she found a book dictating the proprieties of elite when interacting with other elite, those of the same, higher or lower rank. She took this book and moved to a place within the light from the window.

It was interesting reading about the acceptable forms of address within classes and learning how to form propositions for those above and below. There were explanations of relationships past cousin which she had never named before, and shows of affection that were acceptable in public areas. The elite were much more restricted in this sense than servants. There was no restriction on her hugging or kissing her family outside the dining hall, except that it not interfere with performing her duties. Maybe this separateness the elite formed was part of the reason they were able to wager things like spouses on a game. Eve could never imagine her father giving up her mother for anything less than Eve's own life, even his own life.

She started when the post-noon bell rung. She trotted with the book to the shelf she had taken it from.

A male Librarian took it from her. "Next time, put it on the sorting tables at the entrance. We will make sure it is properly replaced."

She nodded, bobbing very quickly. "Yes, sir." She was sure she was replacing it correctly, but she would not argue. Instead she hurried from the library to her rooms. Sarah was just brushing up her uniform when Eve burst in.

"You are still serving?" she asked hopefully.

"As long as I can make it there in time," Eve answered with a smile. She wasn't so late as that and stood with Sarah while waiting for a dresser to fix their hair.

"So where are you assigned?" Sarah asked.

Eve still had no answer for her, so she told her what she could. "It is in the elite section of the Palace. I am to attend with children of the elite."

"Really?!" Sarah said, amazed, but then it was her turn in the chair, freeing Eve from having to explain further.

Eve didn't explain more that night, either, claiming she was tired. In the morning, she went directly to the classroom with the tree on the door, taking her position at the back of the room. No one approached her today. No one looked in her direction more than cursorily. She was glad for that. It was uncomfortable drawing the attention of the elite.

The Ernst began a lesson on the Most High. "The current High One, Bianca, has been in her position since the passing of her mother in 264, when she was raised from Second. Her Second at that time was her husband, Richard. Since his passing in 276, her son, Adam, had been Second. Together they direct and receive direction from the Vinca and Vanto, most of which are relations of one sort or another. For instance, Vanto Albert is the brother of the late Richard. His role is to oversee the relations with our neighbours. Vinca Della, on the other hand, maintains trade with these same neighbours. They work together often, but independently."

And so the lecture continued, through external and internal affairs. The Vanto in charge of agriculture, the Vinca overseeing the Palace proper and working directly with the Headman, the Vanto in charge of upholding the law among the elite. On and on.

The children seemed to lose interest quickly, but this was far more information into the workings of Fontive than Eve had ever been granted before. And it included some history. She had not known the name of the previous High One was Jane, nor that she was the third High One to have this name. She had not known the High One had more than one child. Again at the end of class the Ernst set the children an assignment. To name all the current Vinca and Vanto, their affairs, and indicate which their parents reported to, or their relation to each as the case may be.

After another very quick lunch, Eve grabbed one of her few personal possessions from her room. It was a book of blank pages. She took this with her to the library. Before she began reading a new volume, she found a charcoal and completed the same assignment, circling Vinca Nancy of the Palace as the one she fell under. Her volume today dictated courting practices among the elite; it was an enjoyable read. She flushed a little as she foolishly imagined herself receiving these favours.

Of course, the serving men did not present their intentions the same way. She expected it wouldn't be long before Denis didn't present Sarah with a pink flower, but rather took her hand at the afternoon meal. There seemed an instant connection between the two. He wouldn't offer his coat to her, but would take her pitchers from her at the end of dinner. She could correlate many of the customs, but for some there was no equivalent. A servant did not ask the family of his love for permission to marry her; he simply requested married quarters from the Headman. If she moved in with him, they were married. The elite way was much more formal, but the lower way was no less binding. A couple might divide, but such things rarely happened among the servants. If all the couple wanted was a physical relationship, there were plenty of places for these. Eve doubted a book would tell her if similar activities were conducted in similar ways among the elite.

She almost laughed aloud at the thought. She was still too young to think about having sex herself, but had no lack of information on the topic. She hadn't even been kissed!

She eventually had to tell her friends about her new duties. She explained that she was placed in a room where children of the elite were instructed on decorum. They asked what her duty was, but she didn't know how to answer. She continually told them that she attended. She continued to spend her afternoons in the library, slowly working her way through the shelves. She had moved on from etiquette into histories, reading about the times of various High Ones before Bianca and Jane. This was the sort of information never given to servants. Even the bailiwicks of the various elite were not known to them.

Eve learned of the Princes and Princesses, how they worked with the Vinca and Vanto. The Ducat and Ducati, their positions were roughly equal to Princes; the Princes dealing with internal matters, the Ducats dealing with external, some were actually foreign. More and more history came into the classes, venturing even so far as the Ancient Fall – a time when machines much greater than any still in existence were run with the power of light. There was little available on the subject, though.

Little remained of that time. The Ernst did let some of the Ducat and Ducati relate stories of their visits to the ruins of ancient cities with buildings taller than the tallest trees, many with walls that shone with the sun. Eve would never question even so young an elite as these, but she did wonder if their stories could possibly be true. She tried to imagine how such things could exist. How could one stand a building so high without it toppling itself? The trees used extensive roots to keep from falling. She had watched groundsmen removing a stump once. Could these buildings have roots like a tree? Some structure underground that held them upright? She wrote these thoughts in her notebook along with her new lessons.

She continued to serve at dinner. Her fellow Servers grew more and more jealous of her new duties, which took her from the menial chores they had each morning. They had heard that it involved the elite and wondered why they were not afforded the same honour. Surely their service was in no way less than Eve's. She would have been the first to agree with them – it was not. Although she knew some among her peers were also bright enough to gain as much as she did from her new library access, the most jealous were not among these. Such knowledge would be wasted on them. Her roommates did not ostracize her, though they did wonder why Eve didn't join them in the afternoons any longer.

"Lane wishes you would," one teased her.

Eve blushed. "I do enjoy spending time with all of you; you know that right? But the library," she mused. "I do not know who granted me this privilege, but I would be foolish not to take every advantage it offers. The knowledge, the subjects. It is so much, so wonderful. I wish you could all join me there."

Eve's classes with the young elite continued unbroken for several more months. She learned more of the structure of government, the processes by which the customs were formed and how they might be changed. She also learned a little about Cargon; mostly as it pertained to changes in rank. Rank, honour and any number of other things could be wagered on the outcome of a match. What was not acceptable was a game without a wager. The Ernst was most strenuous on this point.

"You will never *practice* Cargon. You might play any number of lesser games that will prepare you for your first match, but Cargon is the ultimate test of honour. Never feel you must play or accept a challenge. Refusing the challenge is not a loss of face. Losing is."

Eve remembered back to that first night with The High One.

"You must never touch this board. Never touch a piece on it."

She understood even more how critical this was. It was after this lesson that the Ernst approached her for the first time.

"I will speak to you as your instructor. When did Richard pass and what was his relation to the High One?"

"276 and he was her husband and Second."

"What is the role of the Vanto of Diplomacy and who currently holds this post?"

"To engage in relations with other countries. The current Vanto is Albert."

"And his relation to the High One?"

"Brother-in-law."

And so the drill continued. The noon bell had rung several minutes before the onslaught eased. Eve was sure she had answered every question correctly. "And what is the proper response to a Cargon challenge?"

Eve was stymied. That had not been covered in the lesson. "That would depend on the player, and their competence in the Game," she answered finally.

"An acceptable answer. Follow me."

The Ernst led Eve down the hall to another door. This one inlaid with a pair of scales. "You shall report here in the morning tomorrow and every morning after."The Ernst turned and left before Eve had completed her bow. It seemed she had passed the test.

It was ironic that the evening after her lesson on Cargon, there would be another match. This one was between two Ducati. They were both young, perhaps twenty at the most. Eve dedicated a portion of her focus to the game, hoping to learn more about the strategies involved.

Sadly the game was not long. Neither player seemed very sure of herself. Each moved pieces very directly toward the goal, neither moving to protect against the other winning. As a result, the first player was also the first to reach the goal. Eve watched the loser give her ring to the winner.

When the women returned to their seats, a Ducat moved as well. He sat next to the winner now. Eve wondered if a spouse had been wagered or only a betrothed. She hoped for the latter; the former still seemed too bizarre to her. She finished service and did not stay to watch the High One perform her duty to the board. She wanted to be far from the disturbing game now.

"Did you notice the Ducat change his seat?" Eve asked her roommates before bed.

"Yes. Why did he do that?"

"I think he was part of the wager," Eve shared.

The girls gasped. "She wagered her husband?"

"Or intended," Eve suggested, as she still hoped he was. "I think that was what the ring was."

There were more whispers exchanged.

"Did the other Ducati want him and challenge her?"

“Was she trying to rid herself of him gracefully?”

“He seemed handsome enough to me.”

“Why would she accept such a wager?”

“How could he accept the outcome?” Eve asked them. “Would you just go to the one you were handed to like that?”

They all shook their heads. All relationships between servants were voluntary. If one served under another, and the situation was impossible to reconcile, a new duty and position was found. If one were unsuited to the duty they had been assigned, they could be moved to another. It was rare that a servant was pressed into an oppressive duty. There was a level of choice and acceptance to their positions. It seemed not all the elite had this luxury.

CHAPTER TWO

Eve reported to the door with scales and opened it. She found tables spaced throughout the room, holding strange objects she had never seen before. She could not fathom their function. She stepped closer, looking, but never touching them. Some, she thought, she could guess at. There were wheels and gears made of metal as well as glassware in all shapes and sizes. She did not know how they all fit together or what they were used for. She heard the door open and moved quickly to the back of the room.

The Ernst looked at her briefly. Eve glanced from under her lashes at him. He nodded before preparing for his class. He was younger than the previous Ernst, probably not thirty yet. He had black hair and dark skin, dressing in black to complete the somber appearance. He moved to several of the tables setting out slates and chalk.

Then the elite began to pile in. They were older than the previous, ten and eleven years old, only slightly younger than Eve herself. They were dressed similarly to their younger cohorts and stood in pairs at each table. The Ernst reviewed the previous lesson with them briefly.

"You learned that three parts charcoal, two parts sulphur, and fifteen parts saltpetre will make an explosive powder. If I gave you six seeds of sulphur, how many seeds of the other two constituents would you need?" Each pair solved this problem on their boards while Eve did the sums in her head.

"Vanto Damon?" the Ernst asked one of the pairs after a few moments. "Vinca Martina?"

"Nine seeds charcoal and forty-five seeds saltpetre," the Vanto answered.

"Correct. And now you shall attempt to make such a powder. However, as this is somewhat dangerous, you will be using a much smaller amount. Only five seeds saltpetre. So, yes, you will need to divide your seed of sulphur. Use the scales to ensure you have the right amounts."

Eve watched, wide-eyed, as the class went to work. They were using a knife to cut the yellow sulphur into three equal pieces, or as near as they could manage based on their scales. Then, they crushed the black, yellow, and white substances together with a mortar and pestle. The Ernst came and stood next to her at one point. Eve had the impression he would have stood there if she hadn't been in the room at all. It was a good vantage point to see what the students were doing.

"Ducat Herald, not so vigorous. You'll set it off prematurely," he warned. "Prince Gaius, place that mixture in the safe box and leave it. You will have to do the sums correctly if you wish to participate in this lab in future. Excellent, Vinca Martina. That is the perfect grinding method. Look here." He brought the class's attention to the Vinca. She tried to ignore the others and continue her grinding.

"Perfect," the Ernst repeated, holding his hand out for the mortar. He took a pinch of the powder and placed it on the table top. Then he lit a piece of tinder in the fire and touched it to the powder.

Eve screamed when the blast went off. There was a deafening bang and a bright flash. She quickly bowed her head low as eyes found her for the first time. "Eyes front," the Ernst urged. "Now, we shall look at applications for this powder. Any suggestions?"

The elite gave ideas. "Light shows!"

"Warning alarms."

"Crowd control. Especially if they respond like she did." One of the Ducats stuck out a thumb to point at Eve. She kept her head down, blushing now.

The noon bell rang. "I'll ask you each to write down one new use for this powder for tomorrow."

Eve stumbled to the library, skipping lunch all together. She was in shock. They had made lightning and thunder in the room, with a powder! She sought one of the Librarians. "Would you please tell me where I can find information on black powder?"

The Librarian pointed. "Four shelves that way."

"Thank you." She bobbed a curtsy and headed in that direction. The first volume she found held details of horrific accidents in which elite had been marred by the explosive powder. She returned that one to the shelf. She could imagine all too well what damage this powder could do. She tried another; this one detailed different mixes and colours generated by the explosion. Obviously, someone had used the powder to make light shows as had been suggested. She put this one back, as well. The next was not about the powder at all, but one of the constituents, saltpetre. It listed where it was found, other uses for the element, and how it should be stored. She took this and found a seat.

Sarah commented on her odour before dinner. "You smell like you just came out of my father's pipe," she said, holding her nose.

Eve sniffed herself experimentally. She did smell of sulphur; the dust must have collected on her. "I'll run and change. Thank you."

*

Eve turned fourteen while attending the lab. Her friends had noticed her notebook filling and had found her a new one.

Lane also brought her a gift for her birthday. He had learned of it from her friends over lunch. After dinner, he presented her with a pink bloom made from a scrap of cloth. She smiled with delight when she took it.

"How?" she asked.

"My aunt works in the wardrobe, she made it for me to give to you," he said, holding her hand. "And your friends read that pink blooms were a first sign of affection."

"They read my notebook?" she was surprised, not angry.

"A little. Less now that you usually have it with you in the afternoon."

"Thank you very much," she stepped nearer to him. She was a little awkward, unsure just how far this first gift of affection went.

Lane solved the problem for her and kissed her cheek, making her blush. "Thank you, for being a friend."

Eve slipped a few of the teeth of her blue comb through the threads of the bloom, allowing her to wear it during her labs. She removed it before dinner. She wondered if any of the elite noticed her favour. They would know what it meant. Her smile was small, but it remained fixed for the next week.

Her lab lessons included all manner of substances, including mercury - a liquid metal! - as well as copper, gold, steel, and other alloys. She was taught the differences in densities, malleability, and conductance of heat. Imagining all manner of uses for each of these substances, she wrote several pages worth of them in her notebook. Her classmates seemed much less original in their suggestions. Most of their ideas she had found in the books she was reading - accepted uses for the metals. Hers tended to the more practical, such as steel handles on a cooking pot and copper pots and pans.

Eve pored over books containing information on minerals and crystals, books analyzing the composition of various rocks and gems and studies on how to create crystals from solutions. She learned of acids and bases, of melting and vapour points, energy thresholds, combustion. The information seemed limitless. Many of these things were touched upon in the labs, but expounded upon in the written work.

Lessons in the lab expanded to include the use of steam pressure. Watching the steam turn wheels and cogs certainly brought other uses to her mind, and the minds of her classmates — vehicles, threshers, presses for oil and wine. Her imagination expanded as her knowledge did.

She noticed the boys in the class were less careful. She made the move to one table where they were overheating a steam engine, before coming to herself. One Vanto was burned by the steam released, though not badly. Spills of dangerous liquids, slips with knives and scissors – it seemed the elite did not take as much care in their work as the servants. Their haste and lack of caution led to waste and injury. Eve hated to see it.

Beyond her lessons, Eve learned of plants and animals, the workings of the body, the use of nutrients first by plants and then by those consuming plants. She read about medicines, plants, and minerals used for healing. She discovered the sources of dyes and spices, plants of exceeding value. These she did not learn in the lab, but solely from her studies.

The Ernst approached Eve at the noon bell. "Please make black powder using three seeds of saltpetre."

Eve's eyes went wide. She wasn't being asked to answer, but to demonstrate her knowledge. She stepped to the shelf and removed the ingredients. She carefully cut and measured the sulphur and charcoal, using the smallest fractions of both. She crushed them carefully and offered the mixture to the Ernst. He lit the small amount in the mortar, and she only jumped when it banged.

"Take those two samples of ore and determine the identity of each." She went to the two silvery lumps at the table he indicated. She filled a glass jar half with water and put the first chunk in. She measured the water line with a piece of charcoal. Then she did the same with the second piece. She placed both on the scales opposite each other. Then she held each into the flame and determined which heated more quickly. "Nickel, Honoured, and tin," she said with certainty.

"Please assemble the steam engine on that desk." He pointed to another table. She quickly found the valves, pipes, and bolts. She sealed the chamber and placed it on the hearth to heat. In no time, the steam was issuing through the open valve.

"Now, put it to use." That was non-specific. She took the chamber from the fire and closed the valve, maintaining pressure while she thought. She took several cogs, including one with holes the right size for her pestle and built a frame that suspended the pestle over the mortar. She placed one of her sulphur fractions inside and opened the valve. The cog turned, moving the pestle around the mortar, grinding the sulphur, less finely than she had, but sufficiently. She put her head down when she finished and saw the Ernst smiling from under her lashes.

"Excellent. Close the valve and follow me." As she expected, he led her to a new door. This one was enamelled with a golden triangle. She wondered what she would learn through this door. "You will attend here tomorrow morning and every morning thereafter."

He left her before she had bobbed her curtsy. As soon as he was heading into the elite wing, she ran to get some lunch and change her uniform before dinner. She would need to wash as well; the sulphur smell was worse when she handled it herself.

That evening, a match was initiated between a Prince and a Ducat. Eve was distracted from her duty by the game. She did her best to keep the cups full, but often looked up to see the latest move. She nearly overfilled two cups before coming to herself.

She could not afford to make a mistake now; she had come so far. She took a deep breath and shifted her focus back to her duty until the hall began to clear. As there were fewer elite for her to attend, she was able to turn more attention to the game. The two men were very evenly matched, although their strategy was confusing to Eve - it seemed they kept shifting between tactics. She was sure this switching would cost one of them, likely the Ducat.

Another Server whispered to Eve as the night drew on, "Take my table?" Eve nodded with a smile. Eventually, only she and Lane remained to serve the High One, Vanto Albert, and a Ducati who remained with the challengers in the hall. Twice she indicated to Lane that he could leave; she was more than able to serve five alone. He smiled at her and looked away each time. At last, the match ended with the Prince victorious. Eve offered each elite one last cup, but none accepted. She noticed that Lane had already left with his pitchers. She also watched the Ducati, or Princess, as Eve supposed she was now, leave on the Prince's arm. Eve felt sympathy for the woman. Being passed from one to another like that could not be comfortable. Eve wondered if it were possible for her to return to her birth family if her relationships were unsuccessful. These types of exchanges had not been discussed in her decorum classes or readings.

She found Lane waiting to take her pitchers as she left the hall. She blushed a little; certainly he hadn't stayed for this. As he leaned down to kiss her lips, it occurred to her that he probably had. She was flattered.

"What got into you tonight?" he asked. "That was the worst service I've seen from you. Was it because you missed lunch?" he asked her when the kiss broke. Her first kiss.

"No, I was detained by my morning duties, but managed to grab something before dinner," she told him.

"I expected as much." He brushed her cheek with his hand. "You seem uneasy. Is something bothering you?"

Eve looked back to the hall and thought of the Ducati-Princess. She was infinitely grateful that Lane could not wager her in such a fashion. "Just pitying that poor woman," she said quietly.

"Who?" He took her hand, escorting her to her room.

"The Ducati. The Prince won her." Her stomach turned as she spoke the words.

"He won her? Won her over?"

"No, the Ducat lost the match and she left with the Prince."

"Oh... well, you are not her and could never be her."

Even so, Eve dreamed of being passed from Lane to Denis and woke early in a cold sweat. She arrived at the door with the triangle well before the Ernst. Sadly, there was less to examine here. There were no tables, only a ring of chairs. She looked to see if any papers had been left by the Ernst, something to give her a hint of what the class would entail.

Finally, she moved to her place against the back wall and waited for the elite to arrive. The Ernst for this class was very old. His face was deeply lined and the hair he had left was white.

"Oh!" he said with a start when he saw her at the back of the room. "Oh, yes, Server, yes." He took a seat facing her, and she kept her eyes safely lowered. His line of sight to her was blocked as the students came in. They were dressed even more finely, resembling those attending dinner. They were also older – fourteen and fifteen. The oldest boys were likely older than her. She sighed very slightly and risked looking up a little, only to see a Ducat approaching her.

"Are we to have wine with class? That would certainly make it more interesting," he laughed.

Eve bowed, but did not answer.

"Why do you stand back there? Here, you can share my chair," a Prince mocked.

"Let us begin," the Ernst intoned and the students took their seats.

"If the first party is blue and has high status, and the second party is red and has low status, what status is purple?"

What? That didn't make sense to Eve at all. "Middle status," a Vinca put forward. "As purple is both blue and red."

"A worthy hypothesis, Most High. It was not stated that status and colour share a continuum. It is a good hypothesis, though."

And so the class went, the Ernst positing scenarios and the class deriving what they could from the information he presented. Many eyelids throughout the class drooped, but Eve already understood how this type of thinking could be applied to the concepts learned in the lab. If one knew that the different metals' conductance were on a scale based on density, then one could predict a new metal's conductance simply by weighing a sample of known size. If heated vapour produced pressure, applying pressure to vapour would produce heat. She practically ran to the library to begin writing her theories and lessons in her new notebook.

At lunch, Eve found Lane sitting with one of her roommates, Pearl. "I don't know. I thought we were getting closer, but now I'm not sure. I know her duties call her, but I think the library does, too. Can I compete with that?" Lane asked.

"Should you have to?" was Pearl's reply. Eve halted out of sight from the pair. She didn't suspect Pearl was actively trying to turn Lane against her, but she also didn't doubt Pearl had an interest in Lane.

"I don't know." He sounded exasperated. Eve munched her butt of bread while listening to Pearl comfort Lane. Eve pulled the fabric bloom from her pocket and smiled at it. He had made an effort for her. She really didn't deserve it. She tiptoed away.

After dinner, Lane took her pitchers again. "You seem in better spirits today."

"My morning duties were very interesting. I ran late without realizing. Did you have a good afternoon without me?" She hoped her voice conveyed her desire that he had.

"Yes, Pearl kept me company."

"Pearl is good company," Eve told him.

He narrowed his eyes a little. "Yes, she is."

Eve took his hand and squeezed it. "If you would like to chase a less elusive target, I would understand." She took the bloom from her pocket, looking on it fondly again.

He frowned now. "I'm not sure I would like that."

"As you wish," she said lightly, turning her face up for his goodnight kiss. "I will do my best *not* to miss lunch again tomorrow, although I may run late. I will find you."

"That would be lovely," Lane murmured, kissing her. He lingered with his nose against hers and his hands at her waist. "The elusive target is the most satisfying to mark."

She giggled. "Goodnight, Lane."

"Sweet dreams, Eve."

Her dreams were certainly much less disturbing, but also very confusing. Streams of letters and groups, overlapping circles, dividing and redividing items and ideas. She woke feeling less than well rested. She hurried to her class, pinning her bloom in her hair with a comb. She hoped the boys of her class spied it and understood that someone had spoken for her.

To her horror, they took it more as a challenge than a warning.

"A bloom!"

"And not an actual flower – fabric. That's smart. That will keep forever."

"Who would give one to a Server?"

"Hey, Server girl, come sit with me," a Prince offered again.

"Enough!" The Ernst had a dusty voice, but it could still crack like a whip. The students took their seats and class began again.

After class, Eve was approached again, by the same Prince offering her a seat twice before. He was older than most in the class, probably nearly finished. She was worried. The Ernst wouldn't be calling him away now. His family? His friends? Someone would be looking for him, calling him.

"So, Server girl. You have a suitor, and an innovative one. I can't argue with his choice anyway. You are a tasty morsel. I am Prince Louis, and this has to be the worst class. I must wonder who would send you to a class like this?"

"Leave her be, Louis. Let's eat," a Princess called from the doorway. Eve kept her eyes down.

"I'm coming." The Prince leaned into her face for a moment, his lips level with her eyes. Eve held her breath until he turned. She sank to her knees in relief. She had been so close to looking up, so close to retorting to his taunts. It had taken all of her ingrained, practised subservience to resist. She rose slowly and shakily. She had planned to go to the library first, but now she was afraid of what she might write if she did. She ran straight to lunch and Lane.

"What is wrong?" He pulled her aside from the others. "You're pale."

"One of the elite taunted me. I feel stretched," she sighed leaning into him.

"He taunted you?"

"About this," she put a hand to her comb. "They wonder who you are."

Lane smiled at her. "Oh, they do?"

She shook her head, but giggled. The laughter broke her tension enough to enjoy lunch with her roommates and Lane.

After eating, she did go to the library, to write for a few minutes before dinner. She also found the books on logic and philosophy. She didn't know either of these names before finding the books. They were where she expected, on one side of those regarding science. She flipped through a few pages of one on logic before deciding she would need more time to digest it. She returned it to the shelf and found a table to write her notes.

The book on logic helped her immensely as classes progressed. Soon, the Ernst was moving on to questions about the nature of reality and perceptions of it. Eve used his lessons to wrap her mind around their society. The ties binding the elite, or not binding them in some cases. Where would their power be without the serving class? Would they still have some, just less? Where would the serving class be without the elite? Would they continue to work as a unit or fall into disarray without an overarching goal to strive toward? She took these thoughts to her notebook.

If the elite are willing to exchange self for honour, is honour separate from self? She wrote one day. *Do the Serving class have a sense of self if it is not tied to their service? Is their self separate from their duty? What portion is held within each? Extending to the elite, their class obviously holds a certain sense of self, at the minimum in hierarchy.* It was disappointing to know no one would read her ideas, but she did gain satisfaction from thinking the problems though for herself.

Prince Louis continued to taunt her, but she never felt as afraid or as stretched as she had after that first time. He became more of an annoyance than a threat. Constantly complimenting her on her uniform or reminding her that his lap was always open if she wanted a seat. She was sure her non-response would eventually bore him and he would move on to a new target to bully, but he didn't.

Always late to lunch, due to avoiding Prince Louis, Eve took her notebook with her. One day, she was so late that none of her roommates were left when she grabbed her food. She moved to the garden, hoping to find her friends. She spied Lane first. As she approached, she noticed him blush and then saw his hand entwined in Pearl's. She could hardly blame him; she'd been absent for several weeks of lunches.

Eve waved to Lane and Pearl, smiling, but did not come any nearer. After dinner, she walked back to the room just ahead of them. She pulled out her fabric bloom at the door. "Should I give this to Pearl then?" Eve asked.

"No!" Lane was emphatic. Pearl looked a little hurt, and he softened his tone, closing Eve's hand over it. "That was made for you. It was a birthday present. Please, keep it."

"I will, thank you. I wish you both the best." She ducked into the room, giving them privacy.

Pearl came in a moment later. "No hard feelings?" she checked.

"Of course not!" Eve protested. "You are certainly around for him much more than I am. I'll offer this to you again, if you'd rather I didn't have it." Eve pulled out her bloom one last time.

"No, he's right. It means more to you than it would to me anyway."

Eve put it away, making sure she never revealed it in the room again. Pearl would need no reminder that she was Lane's second choice – second, but better choice.

Eve made a point of keeping the bloom fastened in her hair in class. If the Prince would taunt her, why should she stop taunting him? She began fastening it to her robe from time to time, gauging Prince Louis' reactions. At first, he merely approached her, stopping his hand just short of touching the bloom. She would eye him from under her lashes, her head staying down enough to remain proper. He knew she was watching, however, and he would huff and leave.

On and off the pages of her notebook, she contemplated the existence of God. Certainly, she was grateful for her position when it came to relationships, but at the same time, it made everything so difficult for her. Learning from the side, unable to partake in discussions, unable to share her ideas with those who could make them realities. God had certainly put her into a strange position. She began dreaming of herself on the Cargon board. Always blocked from the goal, but always one move from being able to claim it. If only one of those blockers would move aside.

The dream was particularly strong after watching her sixth match. She had been serving wine at dinner for several years. This was another quick and dirty match, another in which a young woman was passed from one man to another. It wasn't surprising her dreams would be haunted with herself on the board, or that she would be taken by the piece which did claim the goal in the end, Prince Louis.

Awaking early from the nightmare, she entered the classroom an hour before the elite students. Even so, the Ernst was there ahead of her. "If a rock is placed in the sea, does the rock become wet or does the sea become rocky?"

Eve smiled, but didn't raise her eyes. This was exactly the sort of question he would ask his class. "Both. The rock joins those on the bottom, making the sea rocky. As well, the rock, having space within, takes in water, becoming wet."

The Ernst smiled at her. "And, if the rock were not porous?"

"Then only the sea would become rocky, as the rock would retain no water upon removal. Nor, if the rock were the only one in the sea could the sea be said to be rocky either. Was this the only rock in the sea?" Only after she asked did she realize she was looking up at the Ernst.

His milky blue eyes shone. "You are a fine student. Take your place," he sighed. Eve heard the students approaching. Today, the Ernst quizzed his students on the nature of time and its flow. Was it even, like water poured from a pitcher, or variable like the wind? Eve imagined it was choppy like water in a stream. It generally flowed in one direction, but it was possible to be thrown back, with memory and dream, to an earlier time, only to be rushed forward again. She made plans to write this after class was complete.

Prince Louis came to her as he had so many times before. He was significantly older than his classmates, making Eve wonder why he was still here. His hand came to rest over her breasts, where she had pinned the bloom today.

"That bloom will never fade. I think his attention is not so constant. But mine is, as you can see." Eve set her teeth at that. She taunted him, but did not seek his affections. Prince Louis put his nose to her hair now, inhaling deeply. He sighed. "Would you taste as wonderful as you smell, I wonder?" His hand traced down her side, just off her skin. It brushed the fabric of her skirt, and she stepped to the side. It was not strictly permitted, but neither was his touch.

He sidestepped with her, grinning now. "Skittish. I like that. Where will you jump to next?" He moved to place his hand on her chest again, and she leaned away to her left, twisting from him. Her skirts brushed his legs. That wasn't permitted either. She backed away again.

He continued to pursue her as she backed herself into the corner. He put his hands to either side of her head, trapping her effectively. Finally, unable to find another response, she turned her eyes level to his. In them she held all of her hatred, her anger, his loss of honour. Would he continue to ignore the impropriety he was inflicting? Would he simply accept the slight she had delivered by staring him down?

He seemed to, showing no offence and instead dipping his nose to her bloom. He was nearly touching her breasts. She tried not to breathe while he inhaled deeply. "Smells wonderful, but I think that's not the bloom. I do wish our stations were not so distant." He pulled his arms away and turned from her.

It had been over a year since the first time he had approached her, but for the second time she fell to the floor in relief. She had nearly spat on him! He would have had her beaten severely for that. She sniffled, and only then realized tears streamed her face. She pulled a kerchief and wiped them away before rising. She took one more deep breath and strode to her lunch with what time remained.

She had nearly forgotten her thoughts from earlier, and it was hardly surprising. She recalled enough to jot them down while she ate. She contemplated getting dragged back into horrid incidents, her confrontations with Louis, the wives and husbands lost, the Cargon dream. It seemed the swells in her stream of thought brought her back to these terrible moments, all of them revolving around the Game. She needed to learn more.

"Excuse me," she asked a Librarian. "Are there any books on Cargon?"

The Librarian's eyes went wide; she hesitated before speaking, "Follow me." The book was in a shelf amidst the histories. *The Rise and Fall of the Mighty* was the title. She would never have known it had any connection to Cargon without the Librarian's assistance.

"Thank you." The Librarian nodded and left her.

The book was not a strategy guide; such things were forbidden. This tome listed some of the most disastrous fates of elite who wagered and lost; the High Ones who fell, Seconds who were lost and replaced. It included titles and lands that were exchanged, spouses and children. She still shivered thinking of such vital things being wagered on any game. There was no history of Cargon played by any but the elite. She hadn't expected one.

She turned to her notebook, all her theories, her designs, and her ideas. They would never amount to anything. She was the only rock in the sea. She could become wet, but she could not make the sea rocky. She had to do something. There had to be some way she could turn her single rock into a mass of pebbles. Some way for her ideas to be spread throughout the elite. Not one occurrence, herself in their classroom, but many tiny pieces. She heard the post noon bell, and hurried to prepare for her evening service.

After dinner, she lingered, watching the High One tend the board. She was surprised when, for the second time, the High One addressed her.

"You return," she spoke to Eve. Eve did not answer. "Your studies progress well; I have been apprised." Eve felt her face flush. Bestowing the honour of instruction on her was great, but to continue to have an interest in her was more than Eve could imagine. "You have a question? Ask." The High One commanded.

Eve longed to ask, "What service can I give when stuck between two worlds? Why do I attend when my attentions are never to be noticed?" Instead she asked her original question, the one that had plagued her since the first night she watched the High One labour at the boards. "Is there no other who could perform this duty? One who understood the importance and took the proper care?"

"There is. I could ask you to do it." Eve gasped, that was certainly too great an honour. The High One chuckled. "It has been done. But the High One who forgets to respect Cargon is destined to soon fall." Eve knew this to be the case, having just read of a number of instances. "This is not the least of my responsibilities, but it is certainly the most ... manual. I find I enjoy it." Her lips curled in a small smile. Eve found herself smiling as well and quickly dropped her eyes again. "Well, child, I have finished for another night. Continue to make the most of what you have been given."

Was that an answer to her unspoken question? Was Eve to take the next step in order to move from one world to the other? Eve dropped her knees and held herself low until the High One had left the hall. Then she turned to the boards, her face now hard.

Make the most of what she had been given. She wanted to take her first step on a road to a new life, a new place. But she had been ordered to never touch the pieces. Her mind warred with her instincts. Her mind was stronger.

Eve took a marble piece in her hand and held it tightly. She could feel every edge, every plane. The corners seemed to bite into her skin. It had very little weight; it was very small, and yet it felt exceedingly heavy, as though she held the world in her hand instead of a tiny piece. Eve placed it on the board in a new position. The movement, she could instinctively tell, was monumental. It wasn't simply the start of a game; it was the start of everything. She had put the world into motion. She turned her back on the three tiered board, walking back to her dorm. From the corner, she saw blue eyes examining her. She ignored them.

*

Adam waited for his mother just outside the hall. She was tending the boards, her nightly chore. One day it would be his charge. He'd never played Cargon. No one had brought a wager worthy of the risk to himself. He had a few minor honours he might wager on a game, but the most obvious to be challenged for was his position as Second and heir.

Adam watched the doors open as his mother stepped out. There was a servant kneeling by the Cargon table. What was she doing?

"Adam, you didn't have to wait for me," his mother smiled.

"I – Would you excuse me a moment?" he asked, slipping past her through the still open door to the hall. The servant had just picked up one of the pieces and held it in her hand. He held his breath. Would she put it back? If she did, he would never mention this – except to her. She must know how dangerous it was for her play with those pieces, what she was wagering – she only had her own life. Surely, someone had told her. She didn't put it back in the starting position. She made a legal move. She knew what she was doing. Their eyes met for a second before she turned and walked away.

Adam stepped back from the doors. "I'm sorry, Mother. There was a servant there. I was just wondering what she was doing in the hall so late."

"Ah, yes. She is bright, that one. I have my eye on her." She slipped her arm through Adam's and led him to their shared suite.

Adam waited for his mother to close the door to her bedroom before leaving again for the hall. Once there, he picked up another piece. He didn't know who the girl was; he didn't know how she knew how to play, but he did not want her challenged by another. He wanted to be the one to win her, the one to challenge her. He admired her bravery. The game had begun.

CHAPTER THREE

Eve pinned her bloom to her chest again before heading to class. The Ernst was there ahead of her again. She dipped in a curtsy before moving to the back of the room.

"Server?" he asked.

"Honoured?" she replied, not looking up.

"If a ribbon is cut down the middle, does it become two ribbons?" he asked.

"Not if the cut is not complete," she answered readily.

He nodded in agreement. Eve wondered if this lesson was also intended for her specifically. If she was given two duties, was she two people? Certainly not, she was already demonstrating that. She pondered this as the class discussed ethics now.

The students had trouble separating laws and customs. There was a difference between the good derived from obedience and that which was independent of laws. Indeed, Eve had trouble with this as well. It was incorrect for her to speak out of turn, but it would have been right of her to prevent the students in the lab from injuring themselves by speaking up. She was forbidden to touch the Cargon board and pieces, but there was rightness in her action last night, she was certain of it.

At the end of class, the Prince approached her once more. She did not look down, but stared at him instead. He hesitated, seeming intimidated. She was right to stop him from stepping on her. She was right to stand up to him. He was wrong if he continued to pursue after she had made her preferences clear.

He only hesitated a moment, though. He put a hand to the wall over her shoulder, and she narrowed her eyes at him. "Lovely Server, allow me to gaze once more upon your beauty." He leered down her dress and lifted his eyes back to her own. He moved to kiss her, and she tightened her lips, making a low growl in her throat. It was utterly unacceptable, but also unavoidable.

He finally flinched and stepped away from her. "Perhaps tomorrow you will accept my affections," he muttered as he left.

Eve adjusted her skirts and went to get her lunch. She detailed her new ethical concerns in her notebook while she ate, contemplating different responses to Prince Louis' advances. She hoped to choose the most appropriate for the next day. She also wrote the Ernst's question down. She was sure she was the ribbon, just as before she was the rock, but the meaning was still elusive.

After eating, she sat with another book - this one discussing the applications of logic to common problems. These were always very hard to understand, using terminology like, "members of the first part, sharing the primary attribute with members of the second part, and members of the third party, sharing the secondary attribute, may be found in relation to members of the first part by way of the tertiary attribute." She would often need to diagram such concepts before she could digest them.

She left a scrap of paper in the book, marking her page, and placed it on the sorting table. The Librarians would not remove it - it was tucked away - but if she returned to this volume, she could find her place. She had seen elite mark their pages in this way.

Eve was at her best through dinner that night. The elite were buzzing over the match that had been initiated.

"Only two moves so far," she heard one Prince whisper to his Princess. A Ducati rose from her table to take a closer look at the board. Eve followed behind her, seeing for the first time the move that had followed her own.

She frowned very slightly. Had the blue-eyed man taken a turn? She hadn't taken a good look at him and didn't know who he was. She couldn't look up and down the tables to find him, knowing he was not seated at hers.

"Who would stop after only two moves?" one Ducat asked his wife.

The Ducati shook her head, looking around for someone to rise and take another move. She would not see anyone do so. Eve would wait until the hall was empty to make the next move. She had begun the Game and she would play it with all the strategy and intelligence she had.

Dinner ran quite late. Eve approached the Wine Master for a refill on both red and white before her tables began to clear. Everyone had hoped to glimpse the players in the Game. The High Table cleared first; the Second and several of the Vanto and Vinca departing. This seemed a signal to the lesser elite that the match would not progress tonight.

The High One did not rise immediately. In fact, She was one of the last to leave. Eve returned her pitchers and visited a moment with Lane and Denis. Both were pleased to see her putting her head back into her duties. Eve peered from the doorway as the High One stepped up to the board. Lane and Denis wished her goodnight, and she waved to them. Eve continued to watch, expecting Her to produce the silk rag and tend the board, but She did not. After a few moments, She turned and left the hall.

Checking over her shoulder, she saw that the other servants were all gone. Eve stepped up to the board and picked up a piece. She placed it in its new place and turned to leave. The sound of footsteps made her spin; the Second was striding up to her. She looked briefly into his blue eyes before dropping into a curtsy and bowing her head.

*

Adam had waited just outside the hall for his mother to leave. He was out of direct sight and didn't think she noticed him lingering. He poked his head back into the hall and saw what he'd hoped. The Server girl was moving a piece. He moved to stand opposite her.

She saw him for the first time when she turned to leave. Perhaps he shouldn't have approached quite so quickly. He'd frightened her; her green eyes going wide before she dropped her head and knees. Adam smiled. She was very dear and genuine in her response.

Adam paused to examine her play before moving a piece of his own. "Are you very tired?" he asked her as she continued to crouch low. "I would not want to take advantage, but it might be nice to play a few turns without all that kibitzing." He waved a hand to the empty tables around them. "What is your name?" he asked. He wanted a name to put to this mysterious young woman.

"Eve," her voice was barely audible, wavering slightly. She was intimidated by him.

"I asked another question, Eve," Adam reminded her. He hoped to put her at ease. He was after all, just a man. "Are you very tired?"

"No, Most High," she said a little louder, a little more steadily. "Not very tired."

She was of, course tired; it was late after all. He would not play more than two or three moves. They each needed rest. "Then rise, and play," he commanded her. "And tell me where and how you came to learn Cargon."

Eve stood, no longer shaking. Something in his voice had steadied her. She looked over his play and chose her response. She moved her piece as she answered him. "I learned here, Most High. I have observed six matches in my time as Server."

Her eyes seemed to turn a brighter green as she played, the green of lawn and grass. He enjoyed being able to look into them. Six matches and she felt confident to play; he was impressed. She certainly hadn't played any of the cursory games the elite did; she knew only what she had learned here. A blush came to her cheeks, and he looked to the board again, making another move.

Adam prepared a way to extricate himself after his next move. She should not play while weary, nor should he.

"I think perhaps this will give the others enough to discuss for another night. You must need rest." He looked into her eyes again and blue began to creep into their color, turning them a sea green. "Good night, Eve." He tipped his head very slightly, less even than he would to an Ernst he played against.

Eve flushed crimson. Adam smirked and almost laughed as she wobbled, sinking into a deep bow. It was unnecessary, but he did understand her wish not to offend him. She was an excellent challenger. As he passed her on his way from the hall, he rested a hand to her shoulder - a sign of service well performed.

*

Eve gasped. Had his touch been warm enough to burn? Or had her nerves simply been on edge enough for it to seem so? As well as hot, the touch was heavy. The weight of the honour she had been given seemed to still rest there as she slowly rose.

Her roommates were still awake when she reached the dorm. "Where were you?" Sarah asked, confused.

"I was delayed. I – I was requested for a personal service," she lied. Perhaps she could claim playing the Second was a personal service to him.

"Personal service? By whom? Everyone left."

"A Vanto returned. He wished to take something from the kitchen with him." The lies flowed out of her, and she felt terrible. Technically, the Second was Vanto, but the only thing he might have taken from the kitchen was herself.

Eve closed her eyes, lying on her back; her thoughts were filled with the board, the Second's blue eyes and his touch. She found sleep very elusive.

It was difficult for Eve to rise in the morning. She arrived at the door with the golden triangle just ahead of the students. She yawned briefly before turning to face the Ernst. She followed the conversation with only a little difficulty and had to hide several other yawns throughout the class.

The topic was ethics, yet again. Eve had begun to formulate her own personal sense of right and wrong, blending the customs she had been taught, the religion she had been born into, and the new knowledge she had gained. This seemed to be exactly what the Ernst was pressing each student to do. She was not ready to write her own ethic, but she believed that she might be after another class like this one.

She sighed as the Prince came to her once more. Today, she had put her bloom back to her comb, hoping to keep his hands from the rest of her. The flower seemed to draw his attention and hands more than anything else about her. She fought another yawn.

"Our Server girl seems sleepy. Late night serving? Who did you serve?" Eve's eyes narrowed on him. The implication was grotesque.

"Yes, it was a late evening," a voice called from the doorway. Eve recognized it and her eyes went wide. Prince Louis' eyes held a question as he turned to see who had addressed him.

"M-most High," the Prince stuttered as the Second entered the classroom.

*

Adam had been leaving a meeting with his mother, when he heard someone addressing a Server. There were few servants in the halls here, and he stopped to investigate.

A junior Prince was pressing himself on Eve.

Adam felt his blood boil. The impropriety, the nerve, and on Eve! That thought should not have come to him. This Server or another, it would be equally inappropriate, wouldn't it? She cast her eyes down, and Adam was sure he saw gratitude in them.

"Perhaps you will allow Eve to be about her afternoon now." Adam stated. Although phrased as a suggestion, Adam's tone brooked no defiance.

Adam recognized the Prince now and nearly growled. Louis turned his eyes back on Eve, full of lust again. Adam's hands balled into fists at his sides. "I look forward to seeing you again tomorrow morning," he breathed into her face. As he turned, she sighed.

Adam watched her chest rise and fall with her sigh. He couldn't blame her for her relief; the Prince was a cretin. "Some elite do not understand propriety. They will find themselves undone by it."

Adam's gaze fell now to the comb in her hair. There was a pink flower pinned to it. Only it wasn't a flower, it was fabric. How ingenious. A bloom that would never fade. Eve shivered slightly as his gaze lingered on her.

"You have an interesting favour there," he pointed to her head. "May I see it?"

She quickly removed the comb and handed it to him. The stitches were fine, delicate, like the bloom itself. Yet no elite would give such a favour to a servant. "This is from another Server?" Adam asked.

"Yes, Most High," her voice was breathy. He still made her uneasy; there must be some way to change that.

"And he still favours you?" Adam asked, handing the bloom back. He wondered what sort of material he might make a favour from, something as durable.

Eve bit her lip. "No. He has... found another, one more... available to him, Most High."

Available? What did that mean? Well, he would press her no longer. "I look forward to your next move."

*

From under her lashes, Eve watched the Second leave. How could she thank him for his rescue? With another move, of course. She stopped at the hall on her way to grab lunch.

Discussion of the match continued through dinner service. Eve beamed as elder Princes and Ducat from her tables praised her moves. Dinner ran late, though not as late as the evening before. The elite no longer expected the players to be revealed. Many speculated on who they might be. A common guess was The High One, Herself. Apparently, she preferred to play in solitude, without an audience. Other guesses included some of the Ernst who might be intimidated by so many observers. None could have imagined a Server might be brave enough to initiate the Game.

Eve noticed the Second leave early from dinner again, although his mother, the High One, stayed to the end, taking a moment to regard the board. Eve found sleep took her much more readily when her thoughts weren't lost in the Game. She slept deeply and well.

In the morning, she arrived in time for her individual moment with the Ernst. "One bloom opens on a tree. Is the tree female, male, or both?"

This was odd; it was a more scientific question than philosophical. "One bloom will not tell. Many are needed to determine if the tree bears both male and female flowers."

He merely nodded and took his seat. Eve moved to the back of the room, still confused. She pondered the question as she had the others. If she were the bloom, perhaps the metaphor could be unraveled. The tree would be her world, but surely she could not actually live in the world of the elite, for all that she trespassed into it.

She held this thought while working out the details of her ethic. The Prince was detained by the Ernst, and Eve was able to slip out without incident. She stopped in the hall on her way to lunch after writing out her ethic, and the Ernst's question, at the library. She had thought the Second hadn't made a move the evening before, but she was wrong.

She looked at the new position of the board and pondered her response. She was just placing her piece when she heard a voice.

"I was hoping you'd come."

Eve started and bowed again. "Please, we are alone. Rise and face me," the Second commanded. Eve complied.

"Well, Eve, I hope Ernst Peter can keep Louis occupied for a few more days."

He had rescued her again. Why would he do such for her? She followed him with her eyes as he came to the board. He wore a dark blue coat and black pants. His boots were soft soled and did not make a sound on the floor. His dark hair curled very slightly away from his head in a carefree fashion. His blue eyes were focused on the board now, but Eve noticed how close he stood to her.

He lifted a hand and it stretched toward her shoulder. Surely he was not thinking of executing the same impropriety he had assigned to Louis? But his hand reached past her to the board and moved a piece. Eve tried to even her breathing, but the tension was not eased.

*

Adam continued to gaze at her rather than the board. Her flawless skin, her shiny flaxen hair, her colour-changing eyes. They were blue today, the colour of the clear noonday sky. Something in this girl attracted him as none other among elite or servants had. He had the sudden urge to curl that arm back to himself and embrace her. He took his own deep breath as she did and let his hand fall, breaking eye contact.

"Your move," he whispered.

She turned and her skirt brushed against his legs very slightly. He saw the blush from over her shoulder, on the skin of her chest. Such contact was taboo, but he was not offended, he was enticed.

He gritted his teeth and closed his eyes, warring with himself, instincts fighting one another.

He opened his eyes when he heard her piece hit the surface of the board. The response, to him, was obvious and he reached for the piece. She was surprised when his arm came over her shoulder, gasping and holding her breath.

Adam placed his piece and knew he must leave. This was wrong of him. He was no better than Louis. "I am making you uncomfortable. I will go." Even as he said it, she sunk into a deep curtsy, seemingly agreeing with him.

*

Eve kept her head down until she was certain he had gone. She didn't trust herself. It would have been too easy to step or lean back into him. The horror of the thought!

Finally, angry with herself, she rose and moved once more. She hurried to have her hair dressed; she would be hungry tonight.

At dinner, the elite questioned the wager when they did not posit players. They imagined something of great importance must be at stake. Perhaps an heir? An estate? Eve ignored these speculations, as she had earlier ones, and attended her duty. Lane smiled at her, glad to see her on level footing. Denis complimented her briefly at the end of dinner before running to Sarah. Eve lingered at the edge between the kitchen and the hall. She watched the High One observe the board before leaving; though again, She didn't tend it.

After She had left, the Second came back into the hall and moved a piece. Why did he wait until She left? Surely he had told his mother that he was playing this match?

"You can come out, Eve. I'm curious to see your response, so that I might sleep on it."

She blushed slightly and stepped from her place at the kitchen door. She didn't duck her head as much as she ought to, but he smiled. She thought perhaps his insistence on her looking up might be ongoing.

*

Adam watched her step into the light. He was taken with her grace as she crossed the floor. As she came nearer, he saw her eyes were green tonight, the colour of jade. She judged the board and his move, responding with her own. A smile played on her lips. She was beginning to be at ease with him. He couldn't be happier. He was so sure he had offended her this afternoon. He smiled back broadly. Her smile widened and her eyes became bluer.

"You are a most interesting opponent," he spoke honestly. "Thank you."

Eve's eyes bulged and she dropped her knees. Adam sighed, nearly groaning. It was easy to see her as an equal across the board but the difference between them was too vast to bridge. He opened his mouth twice to wish her a good evening, but both times the words failed him. They were too lofty, too far from her station, too... elite. At last, he simply turned and walked from the hall.

*

Eve clutched her chest after he had gone. She was sure her heart would beat right out. He had smiled at her. The gratitude had been what dropped her, but the smile was what had made her melt. She dreamed of that the whole night.

Eve arrived in time for another exchange with the Ernst. "A seed falls to the ground. If none witness, will it grow?" This was an existential question; there had been similar asked in the class before. Was there reality with none to experience it?

"The seed will grow, even if only it knows what it becomes," she spoke with sureness, her eyes cast down.

"And if even the seed does not know?" Eve's brow creased. How could a seed not know what it would become? She looked up into his eyes for a moment, the question still on her face. "If the seed is a new plant," he suggested.

She supposed that could happen; plants interbred. "Then it would still have within it what it needed to become that new plant. It would still become itself."

He nodded, accepting her answer. She still didn't completely understand. She was not a new type of person, was she?

The class revolved around ethics once more, and as she had answered this question in her own mind, she focused instead on the questions posed to her these past mornings. She was the rock in the sea. Was she porous? Surely she was. She would take in what came to her in this sea, even if she never made the sea rocky. She was the ribbon cut in two. She had two duties, two places, and she was pulled by both. Would she be cut completely, or could she continue to be both at once? She was the bloom on the tree. The tree could be male or female but without the other blooms, she could not say. She did not describe the world she existed in, the others around her did. She was the seed, unattended; she would still become what she was meant to be.

"Make the most of what you have been given," The High One had told her.

She filed out of the room on the heels of her classmates, giving no heed to Prince Louis and the Ernst.

In the library, she found the logic text she had been studying a few days earlier. Removing the paper marking her place, she tried to determine which party she belonged to, which attribute described her. Eventually, she gave up on this tactic and instead used the logic on her scientific concepts. Volumes of gas, heat, pressure....

*

Adam stopped in the hall after his lunch. She had made another play. He pondered the board; her plays were unique. She blended a number of different strategies into something that was all her own. She balanced defence with attack. She built her position slowly, carefully. She gave attention to each piece individually but never lost track of the whole.

That was the key to Cargon. Focusing on specific pieces left openings for others. Giving too much mind to the overview let the details slip by. And so, as his mother had taught him, ran the country. She used her pawns, the Vanto and Vinca, to tend their daily duties, but she must check each one from time to time to prevent abuse and loss. Likewise, if she focused too long on one, the whole ran down.

Mother was a very good player; for all that she had only played once. She had won his father back from her sister. Richard's attentions had always belonged to Bianca, but his honour was in her sister's hand. She had, in fact, risked the position of Second to win him for herself.

Eve likely hadn't guessed this was his first game as well. No challenger had brought a wager worthy of the risk to himself. She was certainly worth anything it might cost him. He thought he was playing well. Certainly Mother had complimented his plays, not knowing they were his. Well, he didn't think she knew, but she was very intuitive. He would not be surprised if she had guessed he was one of the players. It was impossible she knew the other. If Mother thought his moves were well played, then they most certainly were.

Mother did tell him that, although both challengers played exceptionally well, the initiator was definitely in the stronger position. Looking at the board, he couldn't argue. Eve was certainly narrowing the options quickly, pointing more pieces to the goal while ensuring she never left him an open line. He shook his head, chuckling at his predicament. He would be the first elite to lose to a servant.

Then again, if he won, he'd be the first to defeat a servant as well! He laughed at the inevitability of the situation and made his play.

Thinking so much about Eve had made him wonder if there had ever been a servant raised to the elite. Even if she were only an Ernst, he would be able to court her favour. It was too oppressive for him to try to gain access to her heart when she could not defy him. He headed for the library.

He found the histories and began flipping through indexes and content lists. After a dozen books, he admitted defeat; such a thing had never been done. Common men, those outside the palace - farmers, craftsmen and soldiers - these were occasionally honoured with land and titles for valour and loyalty. But the serving class was different again; they relied on the Palace for their living, they were for all purposes indentured. They were not as independent as those outside. This had kept them from ever breaking into the elite.

He moved to the centre of the room to clear his thoughts before trying again. That was where he found her, bent over a table writing in a book. He was sure it was Eve; she even had that bloom in her hair.

Adam walked up; hoping to see what she was reading and writing. *Pressure on a vapour could release heat rather than requiring it.*

"Pressure without heat?" he asked aloud.

*

Eve thought her heart had just jumped out through her mouth. Her charcoal scratched across her page, over the edge, onto the table and almost into the logic book which still lay open in front of her. She stopped just short of those pages, thankfully. She would never forgive herself if she damaged one of these books. What was the Second thinking, sneaking up on her like that? What was she thinking, thinking of the Second that way?! How did he get so close without her noticing?

The Second frowned seeing the black streak. "Oh," he complained. "I was hoping to read more of that." He pulled the book from in front of her and tried to smear away some of the interfering marks. Eve took her kerchief and quickly removed the mark from the table. "I think I can still read it. Or, perhaps, you would make me a copy? You know what it said, surely."

She nodded, then flushed at her folly. Dipping as much as his closeness allowed, she amended, "It is an honour to serve, Most

High." She dared to turn her head and look at him from under lashes, praying she hadn't offended him.

*

Adam sighed at her response. When he was with her, it was so easy to forget what she was, noticing only who she was. Then she looked at him and he forgot again. Her eyes were green again today. Like evergreen needles, dark, with the barest hint of blue. "Yes," he encouraged her with a smile, "please, look up. And tell me your theory."

Eve licked her lips and looked at the book still in his hands. She took an exposed edge and pulled it gently from him. She looked up at him shyly from time to time as she flipped back to one of her older entries. She read from the page when she found it. "Vapour occupies a volume. As it is heated, it occupies a greater volume, this produces pressure." She took her hand from the book, leaving it open on the table. She looked directly into his eyes now. She spoke quickly, though. It seemed she was still uneasy with him. "It stands to reason that if you reduce the volume the vapour occupies, you would also increase the pressure."

"And produce heat," Adam finished for her. "That is very clever." Eve continued to stare at him as he started to ramble. "It should be fairly easy to test. The most difficult part would be finding a vessel that can be compressed while remaining sealed. I will speak with Ernst Derek about this. He may have some idea what vessel to use." Adam was lost in these thoughts and started to turn from her.

*

Eve was a little relieved when he turned away. She was certain he could see every thought she had ever had, and the ones about him would definitely be offensive in the extreme. Even so, he had accepted her theory; he wanted to test it. She craved his attention, but perhaps it was possible to have too much. His eyes could be too intent on her. Her idea could hold his attention for a while instead. Her relief was short lived.

"You come here most afternoons?" the Second asked, half-turned toward her.

Eve nodded again, too surprised by his sudden return to speak.

"Good. I will see you here tomorrow. Bring your writings," he called as he walked away. The elite and Librarians looked at her and she bowed her head, blushing. What could she tell them? What did they think? Had she offended them? Had she offended the Second?

As the eyes around her returned to their reading or duties, Eve took a breath to calm herself. She pondered what had just happened. Cargon *had* changed the world. Her writings were going to be read by the Second. They wouldn't be wasted in the corner of a servants' dorm. He was going to share them with an Ernst and act upon them. She felt like dancing for joy.

She quickly finished up what she had been working on and returned the book to the shelving table. She headed outside and began twirling under the trees, singing as she did. She felt wonderful; she felt fulfilled. She was the seed and someone was going to witness her grow!

Lane came and grabbed her by the waist, spinning her around. Then he twirled her into Denis who also revolved her once. The two laughed at her shocked expression.

"Well, we could hardly let you dance alone," Lane muttered. He turned Pearl around now and passed her to Denis, taking Eve's arm once more. She laughed aloud, taking Sarah's arm and turning with her. She danced with her friends until the post noon bell.

Eve took her place at dinner with pride. She was serving both her duties now. Like the divided ribbon, she was twice as long, twice as effective.

She noticed a piece had moved since the previous evening. The Second had made a play this afternoon. She contemplated her reply through dinner, the meal providing ample time. Dinner ran long again, the elite taking time to discuss the game, the players, the moves, the strategies.

As she had every night this week, she remained until the last elite left, regardless of how many lingered at her tables. Eve's friends had started to notice.

"Why are you sticking around here, Eve? Everyone has gone; even the High One is gone," Sarah asked. That wasn't strictly true. The High One had also stayed behind, taking individual time with board.

"I... I must, all right?" She hated lying to her friend.

"You have a duty?"

"Well, no, I have... a meeting," she lied.

"Oh! Well!" Sarah smirked. "We won't expect you soon then," she teased, assuming this must be a romantic meeting to be so late in the night. Eve blushed thinking of such a meeting with the Second. It was made worse when she looked out and saw the mother of her affections still studying the board.

Finally, the High One nodded to herself and departed. Even so, it was several minutes before Eve was able to straighten herself out enough to remember Cargon at all. By this point, the Second was waiting for her at the Cargon table.

*

Adam knew Mother suspected him now. She had practically looked right at him in the entry when she left the hall. He had tried to be discreet, and so she did as well. But she had definitely marked him. He tried not to think about that and entered the hall again. It was time for another meeting with Eve. Another night over the board. Another night of forgetting what she was and only pondering who she was, how brilliant, how lovely.

She wasn't there when he entered; at least, he didn't see her at first. Eventually, he spied her at the door to the kitchen, in the shadows. He wondered why she hadn't made her move yet, very few options were left. He approached the table to await her. When she emerged, she seemed flushed. What had she been thinking?

"I think you might have me now," he admitted. His mother had pointed out some of the likely plays and counter plays that could come from this position, and almost none of them favoured him.

Eve smiled as she moved her piece. Her eyes were blue, almost the shade of her dark robe. He still didn't understand how they changed or why. Her play was one his mother had predicted so he moved as soon as she released the piece. Her response was as quick as his own had been. There were fewer and fewer safe paths for each of them. They played several turns at that pace, each moving a piece immediately after the other. Then he heard her gasp and saw her broad smile. It was dazzling. He had to tear his eyes from it to the board.

He cringed very slightly; he had erred in his haste. She had a clear path to the goal now. She claimed it with exultation, her face glowing with pride and satisfaction. She had been lovely before, but she was undeniably beautiful now. She took his breath from him. It was a full minute before he came to himself enough to round the table to her.

He pulled the Second's crest and its chain from his neck. Careful not to disturb her hair, he slipped the chain over her head. As he settled it, the back of his fingers brushed her collarbone. His breath caught, and he was sure hers did as well.

Her lips parted slightly and her eyes fluttered shut. She had her face turned as though for a kiss. That couldn't be what she wanted, could it? It was certainly what he wanted, but it was too soon. She couldn't know yet, could she? Adam's hand rested just off her cheek, and it took determination to pull it back. He cleared his throat, turning to the board and resetting the pieces.

Eve opened her eyes again, and she moved to help him with the board. She reached for the same piece at the same time that he did and touched his hand. She bowed her head and flushed.

Adam felt as though something had flashed up his arm when her fingers brushed the back of his hand. She was instantly real to him. He had to touch her again. He grasped her hand before she could pull it back, although she had diverted her eyes. He pulled her hand to himself, turning her to face him. He put the back of her hand to his cheek. Then he turned slowly toward it, smelling the soap, the silver polish from the pitcher, and underneath both, her. Her palm was against his and he could feel small calluses. Hers was not the hand of a courtesan.

Eve met his eyes, looking to her hand against his cheek. He moved his lips to her hand now. Adam gazed once more into the deep blue pools of her eyes and then forced himself to let her go. She needed time; he needed to give her time.

"Until tomorrow, Eve." His voice sounded harsh to himself. He hoped she didn't hear some threat in them, but he didn't trust himself with her any longer tonight. He turned and left quickly, although he should have finished resetting the board. He didn't have the strength to resist her that long.

*

His husky voice had taken what little breath she had left. If she dared to dream it, she would imagine he wanted her as much as she wanted him. That was impossible. Still, his warm touch on her hand, his kiss there. It had made her head spin and her heart falter. Just when she thought she was to be punished, she was blessed instead.

Eve stood in shock for a long while. When her brain finally found itself again, she turned to the board and finished resetting it before walking slowly back to her room. She let her hand trail on the wall for support, still feeling very light. Was she walking or was she floating?

The lights were out when she returned to her dorm. She undressed and hung her uniform blindly, reflexively.

"You are late," Sarah teased.

Eve blushed and thought Sarah must be able to see it even in the dark. "Yes. He was... well, he was all that and more," she said unable to answer properly.

"Mmmm. You will have to introduce us. Tomorrow, maybe?"

"Maybe," Eve answered noncommittally. How could she introduce her fellow Servers to the Second?! How could she still be thinking of him that way? What would they say? What would he say? Impossible, simply impossible.

Despite the impossibility, she lay on her mattress with her eyes open, seeing his smile, imagining his kiss. She toyed with his medallion all night.

CHAPTER FOUR

Eve dressed quickly just after sunrise, pulling her dress over the medallion. She didn't want to have to explain its appearance to her roommates. She wondered if the medallion had special significance. She thought to check in the library as she pulled on her robe.

She made sure to bring her old notebook with her today. The Second had asked her to bring her writing; he might want to see some of the older entries as well. She thought they were unlikely to be of interest to him, being about the elite and their relationships. These topics were no doubt as well known to him as the servant hierarchy was to her. She did have her first notes on crystals and minerals at the back though. There were uses for black powder and other materials.

She grabbed a quick breakfast along her route and was in the room ahead of the Ernst for the first time in a while. When he entered, his voice raised slightly, "The pawn moves at the masters' command. If the pawn falls who holds the blame?"

Eve moved nearer so that he need not raise his voice for her. "The opponent," she answered with a smile.

"Smart. Smart," he chuckled to himself. "It has been long since I was outwitted by a student. I do wish you were in one of these seats."

Eve bowed low at the honour he gave her. "I wish the same, Honoured." Then she took her place at the back of the room.

The class followed the Ernst's original intent, talking of the dilemma faced by one given a command against conscience. Eve listened with interest. It was a conundrum. After all, systems only worked properly if the parts followed the dictates placed on them. Independence, however, gave one the option of operating counter to that dictated, and in some instances the responsibility to do so; in the case of preventing greater harm to the system itself, for example. Eve prepared to write these ideas when she reached the library.

She quickly wrote her thoughts, fighting yawns with every other word. Her eyes started to drift shut. She had gotten almost no sleep the night before. She put her head on her arms and dropped her charcoal.

*

Adam entered the library with a bounce in his step. *Day one*, he thought. A fresh start. He was ready to begin his courtship. He had a gift in his pocket even.

He found her leaning on a table with her head on her hands. Had she fallen asleep standing up?

"Sweet dream?" He stepped up behind her.

Eve's eyes flew open. Startled, her books flew off the table. She was blushing furiously as she ran to retrieve them.

Adam chuckled as she flailed out in surprise. That hadn't been very nice of him, but he hadn't thought she was actually asleep. He bent to pick up her book even as she came running to it. He didn't give it to her right away, opening the notebook instead as he straightened. She rose as well, holding the other one.

Adam started at the beginning of the book. A discussion on the various elite and their roles. The courtship practices — he knew she knew of those. He looked to her then and saw her listing to one side as she fell asleep upright again. How tired was she? Did she sleep at all last night? He couldn't deny that she had filled his mind for longer than was appropriate, but he had eventually wandered off into dreams, where she featured prominently as well.

He kept a hold on the book in his hand and took the one from hers before she let it fall. Then he ducked under her arm, and her head brushed against his cheek. He was thankful there were so few others in the library today; this was a little more contact that was strictly proper. He smiled at having her so close, and it being acceptable to do so; it was wonderful. He put an arm around her waist and backed a few steps to one of the chairs. He shifted her on his lap so that he could move the books to his other hand. Her head was tucked under his chin now. He looked down to see that she was still asleep, still comfortable. She hadn't even twitched. When no one was looking, he kissed the top of her head and opened her notebook again.

He was glad to have all afternoon. He had to reread several sections and flip back occasionally to read older entries. She believed the elite *took* people wagered in Cargon? Of course, this wouldn't have been laid out in any books or lessons. The relationships among the elite were never as simple as blood and marriage vows. How little she understood of these things, but how much she understood of others.

Science, for example — she seemed to grasp every idea as soon as presented to her. Not only understand, she was able to adapt her theories on density, pressure and crystallization. It was undeniably inspired. Her suggestions for uses of various materials were incredibly practical. This was hardly surprising given who she was and where she came from; nothing of the sort would have occurred to himself or another of the elite.

It was obvious at which point in her notes she moved from science to philosophy. Her writings grew much more profound. Her views on herself, her society and his. Her personal ethic. He was learning so much of her and from her. He wished he could give her back a part of all she had just given him. It was as though her thoughts and feelings were being transferred directly from her head and heart into his while she lay against them. He rubbed his cheek against her head once more as he neared the end.

Ernst Peter, he thought with a chuckle. You test her even more than you did me. A rock in the sea? And not only had she answered his query, she had turned it into a personal message. The ribbon, where had the old man dredged that one from? Once more, she had managed to find herself in the unsolvable problem he posed. The tree had him at a loss. There were male and female trees? He didn't even know of such things, but apparently Eve did, as did Peter. He would have to ask Eve about that one.

He felt a shifting on his lap and smiled broadly. She was waking. He could thank her for all she had given him while she slept.

*

Eve woke somewhere warm and soft. She wasn't lying down though; she was sitting. She opened her eyes slowly, taking in the library. She must have fallen asleep in one of the chairs, but she didn't remember any of them being padded. Rising to her feet, she saw the boots behind her slippers.

Her eyes went wide. She had been sitting *on* someone. As she continued to wake, she remembered who she'd been speaking with when she drifted off, the Second. She had been in his lap, her head on his shoulder. She yipped, mortified. She sank low and flushed deeply. She could not be spared punishment for this. Falling asleep? And then... she tried to fight the tears building in her eyes.

Eve shivered, awaiting an axe to fall on her neck. None came. As her mind continued to work, she noticed the angle of the sun through the window and its redness. She jumped up and ran from the library.

*

Adam was confused. What had gotten into her? There had been nothing improper in her actions and very little in his. Why was she lowering herself now? He thought back to her writings. She knew about rank and Cargon... surely she understood.

She spontaneously jumped up and ran from the library. Adam was confounded now. First she lowered herself, and then she ran away? She'd forgotten her books. It didn't make any sense at all. Unless, she really didn't want his attentions. Perhaps that was it. His chest suddenly felt very tight. He closed the books, still intent on showing them to his mother and Derek. Regardless of her feelings toward him, her ideas needed to be shared.

*

Eve narrowly avoided colliding with several servants in her sprint. She dropped her skirts and started twisting her hair into some of the coils that would be needed. She held these separate sections as she ran. She must look a total fool, she thought as she plopped into an empty chair at the dressers', Bonnie's. None of that mattered, only that she made it in time.

"Please!" she begged.

Bonnie chuckled and sighed. "Well at least you have it started. I will try to get you out there in time." Bonnie was as good as her word. She wound the sections deftly and pinned them neatly. "You will still need to run," she warned even as Eve burst from the chair and tore out of the room.

She skidded to a halt before the Wine Master. He squinted at her for a moment. She took one very deep breath and then returned to gasping for a few. Then she took a second deep breath and found her breathing evening out. He nodded very slightly before giving her the pitchers.

She walked as quickly as she dared to her position. She was in place only seconds before the elite entered. Lane looked at her in disbelief. She saw others around the room smirking. They were certain she would be assigned a new duty tomorrow. Tardiness was not tolerated.

Eve put every thought thereafter into her duties. She couldn't risk anything or anyone distracting her. She must make the rest of tonight's service as flawless as possible.

The Second entered the hall beside the High One. "The game has ended," she commented as they passed the Cargon table.

"So it has," he said. Eve saw him mark her before taking his seat.

Whispers filled the hall. The game was over, but everyone was still in their places. Who had lost an honour? Who gained? It couldn't be something minor; the game had been so slow and secret.

The first course came and went while the elite continued to speculate and find no answer. The High One put them out of their misery. "Second, where is your father's honour?" She asked in a loud clear voice.

Eve gripped her pitchers more tightly. His father's honour? What did that mean? What did she have around her neck? The medallion suddenly felt much colder and much heavier where it was nestled under her dress. Only a few links of the chain showed on her chest.

"I'm afraid I lost it," the Second admitted boldly. His voice carried in the now hushed hall. The elite were looking amongst themselves again, trying to find the bearer of the Second's crest.

"And you could not have given something lesser?" The High One asked in a quieter voice as the whispering picked up in volume. She pointed to the many honours pinned to his coat.

"She deserved nothing less," the Second assured the High One.

She raised Her voice again, speaking with authority, "Then tell me, Vanto, who has joined our family?"

Vanto? Eve thought with confusion. He was Second; he would only be Vanto if... She paused in the middle of a stride. If another were made Second... It couldn't be. It wasn't possible. Her brain refused to accept even the peripherals of such a concept.

Eve saw the Second rise and momentarily considered running for the kitchen. She had even started to move in that direction, reaching the edge of one of her tables when he came to her. She shook as he faced her and dropped into a very deep curtsy. This couldn't be happening. This was a punishment, a very special, very honourable punishment for a servant who had given such great service, but had stepped so badly she must be removed. Her brain sought to put reason to the situation.

*

Adam cringed, watching her base herself again. She didn't understand. He was rightfully lowered for not seeing to it that she was aware. He was sure, with all her studies, that she would see what she had won. Of course, none of those around him understood either. He took her pitchers and put them on a table. Her hands fell as soon as they released the silver. Adam sighed and put his hands to her bodice, slipping his fingers under the bits of chain exposed there. She gasped, and he made a note to apologize later. This was necessary for the moment.

He lifted the medallion from under her dress and let it fall over her chest. There were gasps around the room. "Rise, kin," he said quietly. It was easily heard through the room, but Eve needed the order to make her move. She was still in shock. How could he have let this happen?

Offering his hand, he felt relief when she took it, rising. The shock on her face was clear, but she was moving again. It would take time, but she would understand. She had taken his hand and so wasn't revolted by him. Even now she leaned on him slightly, as though afraid of falling.

Leading, keeping her close to his side, he stopped before his mother. "Mother, may I introduce Eve?"

Eve paused, eyes popping, but finally bowed her head slightly, cheeks flushing red.

Adam relaxed a little at Eve's nod. She was starting to accept; she was starting to understand.

The High One rose. "It is wonderful to finally meet you, Eve," she said with a broad smile. Finally? Adam thought. She knew Eve? Of course, he thought with sudden realization. Someone had put Eve into Ernst Peter's class. Bianca was far more intuitive than even Adam had given her credit for. She took Eve's hand in welcome.

Adam nearly fell as Eve's weight was suddenly full on him. He smiled at his mother and chuckled. She turned to the hall. "Please, be about your meal. We will make a place for our new kin."

Bianca turned a chair for her son, and he sat in it lying Eve over the arm. He put a hand to her cheek. She wasn't flushed any longer; she wasn't clammy. That was good.

"Just fainted," he assured his mother.

She nodded. "Hardly surprising." She dipped a kerchief into her wine and put it under Eve's nose.

*

Eve's brain raced even when her senses had stopped taking anything in. Kin? She was not their kin. What was she? Who was she? She had known when she picked up that piece that the world would change, but she had never guessed how much.

She had felt treasonous merely nodding to The High one. She had been overwhelmed by Her pleasure upon meeting her, officially, equally. It was simply too much, and yet... something was drawing her out, a scent... wine.

Eve blinked slowly, looking at the ceiling of the hall. She had not seen it often; it was in need of dusting.

"Oh good, she's coming around," the Second informed his mother and began propping her up.

That was when Eve realized she was sitting on the Second, the Vanto, again. She flushed and put a hand over her eyes, trying not to think.

"No one is surprised at your reaction," he told her. "There has never been elite such as you. It must be very confusing."

Eve tried focusing on his blue eyes. Perhaps that would help. If she could cling to one thing in this whirling world, she might be able to make it stop spinning. She licked her lips while looking at his rose coloured ones.

"So, what am I to call you now?" she asked when she finally found her voice.

Adam smiled broadly, happy to answer this question. "Adam."

"Not Brother?" she asked with a sparkle in her eye. "Vanto Adam?"

He laughed quietly. "We are not usually so formal within the family, but you may, if you prefer. Are you ready for some more introductions?" He put his face a little nearer hers.

She could smell his breath again; he had not had any wine. Still unable to think straight, her breathing and heart seemed regular enough, but her head was still spinning. "Not quite. But I might be once I am standing."

He tossed his head back as he laughed this time, and Eve thought she had never heard such a wonderful sound. "Certainly!" He kept one hand on her hip and another on her hand as he helped her to her feet. He held her in the crook of his arm for a moment until he was certain she was steady. He turned her to the line of Vanto and Vinca at the next table.

"Ready?" he asked, his lips next to her ear. His breath there made her tingle.

"I believe so." Eve tried to lock her knees and make her legs gel by taking one more deep breath. He kissed her just under her ear. Eve closed her eyes as the world whirled again. "Oh that doesn't help," she whispered. Her eyes opened wide and she covered her mouth, astounded by what she had just said.

The High One swatted his back, but Adam laughed regardless. "I suppose not," he agreed. He pressed her hip to start her moving, and they approached an auburn-haired Vinca. "Eve, this is Della, our cousin."

Eve reflexively bent her knees, but Adam held her up against him. *Right*, she thought, *this is going to take a while to get used to*. She nodded instead.

"A pleasure," Della spoke directly. Eve didn't trust her voice, and Della didn't seem to require an answer. Adam shifted her to the next pair.

"And this is Albert, our Uncle, and Maria." Eve did only nod this time, although she also blushed. It felt wrong. Surely she wasn't doing this right. They must all be terribly offended. A Server treating them as equals. Adam didn't let her stop, though; he moved her along the entire table. When that was finished he took her to the Vinca and Vanto at the table on the opposite side of the High Table. She was grateful she already knew their names and relationships because she could barely hear Adam for the blood rushing in her ears.

*

Eve was doing much better after four or five introductions. Adam didn't have to push her nearly as hard for each following place setting. At every nod her colour flushed, and he worried she might faint again. He was glad to return to their seats. Someone had brought another chair. As much as he would have enjoyed her in his lap, this was preferable. She didn't seem to think she should have the seat between him and Mother, though. He almost had to press her into it.

They had missed one whole course, but she would have ample time to eat now. Provided he could convince her to do so. His mother began chiding him as soon as they were both seated again. "You didn't tell her? She didn't know she was Second? You should have given a lesser honour. The poor girl is going to faint again."

As she said so, Eve's eyes rolled back, and Adam slipped an arm around her shoulders so her head could fall onto his chest instead of the table or chair. "I thought she knew." He pulled out her notebooks. "She knew about rank and Cargon, as well as my position. I didn't realize how little she understood."

Bianca began flipping through the pages. Adam stopped the Server from taking Eve's plate; she needed to eat.

"She is confused about our associations, isn't she?" his mother mused.

"Quite. She is also patently brilliant. You chose well," he teased his mother now.

"I?" she said slyly. "I chose nothing. I just gave a young servant who was able to grasp Cargon, after one match I might add, the chance to use what God gave her. *She* chose to challenge you."

"Actually, she didn't challenge me. I don't think she had any idea what she was doing that night, but I couldn't very well let one of those have her." He nodded his head toward the elite farther down the hall.

"Of course not," Bianca said knowingly, lifting a piece of her dessert to her mouth. "Ah, here she is again," Eve had started blinking again. "Eve, please, eat." Bianca put her own fork to the girl's mouth and she ate the fruit on it.

"Thank you, Most High."

Bianca rolled her eyes. "Bianca," she insisted. Eve's eyes were huge and Adam worried she might faint again.

"How about Mother, then?" he suggested, putting honour into it, so she might accept. Her mouth opened and closed several times. He took one of them as an opportunity to put a piece of pork in it. She chewed and swallowed before trying again.

"Mother?" she said tentatively.

Bianca smiled. "Yes, I do like that. That will be fine. Now, eat. You will never stay conscious if we don't get some food in you."

How very motherly, Adam thought, but the tone seemed to have worked. Eve began working away at her pork, then she ate her dessert and his. She didn't touch her wine, which he thought was for the best. He did ask the Server to find some juice.

*

As the elite began to depart, many of the Princes and Ducat came to introduce themselves to the new Second. Eve nodded to all of them but tried to think about her new position as little as possible while she ate. They were right; she needed food for her brain to continue to function in any capacity. At last, it was just the three of them left in the hall.

"You still do not believe, do you?" Mother asked her.

Eve shook her head. She looked from the High One, Mother, to Adam and back. Their faces both encouraged her. Eve noticed her books on the table in front of Mother. She had been reading them. Looking around the room, she pondered how different it looked from this spot. Had the world moved, or just her? She would have to ask the Ernst. She would be able to ask the Ernst, she thought with a big smile.

Mother pulled the undyed silk from her pocket. "I would not ask a servant," she held it out to Eve, "but I am pleased to ask my daughter."

Eve took the cloth and rose smoothly. She tended the board in the same ritualistic manner she had watched Mother do so many times before. She ensured every speck of dust was gone. It felt so good to serve.

When she was half done, she asked Adam and Mother who stood behind her, "Am I to go unpunished for breaking your order?" They both creased their brows in confusion. "You told me to never touch these pieces," Eve reminded her.

Mother laughed, and it was only slightly less lovely than her son's. "That was hardly an order. Merely a warning. One I am glad you didn't heed."

Eve finished her duty with a full heart.

"And now I have a rather embarrassing admission," Mother told Eve. "My son," she looked at him pointedly where he stood on

Eve's other side, "was negligent in informing me of your joining us. I'm afraid your room is not ready. It will be for tomorrow, I assure you."

"My room?" Eve was confused, she already had a room.

"Yes, well, maybe we'll just deal with that tomorrow, then," Mother finally murmured. Adam looked confused. Eve felt confused.

Eve bowed to both of them and Adam caught her. "No more of that," he muttered, catching her by the arms. "I bow to you now," he said bending further than he had before.

The High One grabbed her son's arm and righted him. "Sleep well, Eve," she said pulling Adam after Herself. "She needs to sleep on it," she whispered to him just before they were out of earshot.

Eve stood for a moment after Adam and Mother had left. Then she shook herself. She was falling asleep on her feet again.

She laughed. She still was asleep! It was so obvious, why hadn't she noticed before? Of course, it was still a dream. She hoped waking in her own bed would cure her.

Eve's roommates were still awake when she arrived. They all curtsied low as she entered.

"Oh, please," she muttered. "This dream is too much. You all are acting absurd." She shook her head and began removing her uniform.

"Eve?" Sarah asked, looking up. "Are you all right?"

"Well, I'm asleep on my feet, so I don't think I'm quite *all* right, but I seem to be ready to wake up."

"Eve, you are awake," Pearl tried to assure her. "You were taken to the High Table."

She laughed and smiled at her friends, "Yes, of course I was, and the Second kissed me on the lips," she said in jest. He hadn't done any such thing.

"If you say so," Sarah said with a smirk. "Apparently that was the reason you were lingering after dinner. Your secret meeting?" She tittered.

Eve sat with a thump on her mattress. He hadn't kissed her passionately. If it had been her dream, wouldn't he have done so? Certainly almost all of her dreams had included that. She put a hand to the medallion on her chest. She had definitely been awake when she was given this, when she won. Looking more closely at it, she saw it was shaped like a lion's face and mane. What did it mean?

"Eve? Do you believe you're awake now?" Pearl sounded concerned.

"I'm... awake? That, all of that, really happened?" She felt tears in her eyes. Shock and disbelief racked her. She felt very cold all of a sudden and began shivering uncontrollably. Sarah laid her down and climbed on her mattress with her, wrapping herself around Eve to warm her up.

"Eve? It's all right, Eve. You're going to be all right." Sarah tried to soothe her, but Eve's mind couldn't wrap around it. Eventually, exhaustion got the better of her, sleep claiming her.

Eve dressed in her uniform in the morning. Her friends eyed her curiously but didn't speak.

"Well," she said finally, "I'll see you at dinner." She gave them a small wave.

They exchanged curious looks. Then Sarah came and hugged her before she could open the door.

"Goodbye, Eve!"

Eve hugged her friend, confused. "I'll see you again, Sarah."

"Right, of course." She wiped her cheeks.

"Give Lane and Denis my best," she said as she opened the door. The Headman stood in the hall. "Oh!"

"Good morning, Most High. Please, follow me." Eve glanced back over her shoulder. Her friend met her eyes for the last time and they teared over. She blew Sarah a kiss and followed the Headman into her new life.

"Is it true? I am Second?" she asked him, knowing he would never joke about something like this.

"Yes, Most High. I am escorting you to your new quarters. The High One suggested you might wish to change and attend your morning class. She believes keeping as close to your previous schedule would be best."

"Yes." She would be able to participate in class now. That would be very interesting, but surely she still had a duty to attend, not simply class. She really had gleaned most of what she could from it. "What is Adam... um Vanto Adam, doing?"

"He is in council with Vanto Albert, Vinca Della and the High One," the Headman answered.

"Shouldn't I be there?" she asked, still completely unsure of herself.

"They would welcome you, should you choose to attend, but insist that you need not rush into your new role. Vanto Adam will continue to council until you are ready to join them." He smiled at her without meeting her eye. Eve smiled back; he was very practised at this.

"Well, I shall follow you for now," a small laugh escaped her lips.

"Here we are, Most High."

"Is it possible to not call me that, at least for today? It still doesn't sound right," she requested.

"As you wish. There is a change of clothes for you. If you require assistance, I can send for Betty. She will be at her morning meal now after seeing to the Vanto and High One, but she will be happy to Serve."

Eve laughed. He wasn't offended. "I'm sorry, but I do believe I can manage to dress myself." She laughed again, more loudly now, and was happy when he chuckled with her. It did seem absurd. Gathering her breath, she had a more pertinent question to ask. “Where am I to attend the noon meal?”

“Ah, yes. I believe Vanto Adam was planning to meet you outside class. Should you decide to spend the day elsewhere, I will let him know.”

“No, that will be fine. Thank you, ummm. What do I call you?” she asked in a whisper.

He smiled and chuckled, “Henry.”

“Thank you, Henry.”

“If I may?” he offered, and she nodded. “Try to avoid other servants for the first week. You will put them off very quickly, they won’t know what to make of you.” He laughed again.

She joined him. “Indeed! Oh, but I will have to visit two. Perhaps I should do that before I change,” she mused, looking at herself and tucking the medallion under her shirt.

“Your parents?” he suspected.

She nodded. “I will have to say goodbye.”

“You will be able to find your way back? Would you like an escort to the grounds?” Henry checked. She was much more stable now than when he had met her this morning, but this was all very new still.

“An escort to the stable would be perfect, thank you.”

“Try not to thank me so much,” he whispered to her. This was what he meant about putting off the servants.

“Right, of course.” He was already on his way out the door as she muttered.

She paid more attention to the route as Henry led her to the stable. Peeking in the door, she called, “Hello?”

“Up here!” her father called from the loft. “Well, it will definitely be latrine service for you after a morning here,” her Pa warned her as he descended the ladder

“No, Pa. It will never be latrine service for me,” her voice broke. “You won’t have heard, of course. This sort of news doesn’t spread through us as quickly as them.”

He looked down at her now, worry on his face. "Heard what? What happened? Is it the High One?"

Eve shook her head. "She is fine. She is better than fine. She... she has a new Second."

"Her son; something happened to her son."

"No, Pa, listen. She... he... he lost his place. He wagered it and lost it to another."

"What? How does that happen?"

"That's not important, Pa. Well, I suppose it is. There is an elite Game, and I played it."

His eyes went wide with sudden comprehension. "You are the new Second?" He dropped his eyes instantly, "Apologies, Most High."

"No, Pa, no. Please. I'm still your pretty. I'm still your daughter. Look at me?" she half begged.

He didn't look up. She squared her shoulders. "Look at me," she commanded now. It felt so wrong, but she needed one last word with her father.

His eyes were filled with fear now. "You will tell Ma, and the family. You will let them know? I can't go to the kitchens, I can't tell her there. I wish I could say goodbye properly." She felt tears sting her eyes. He still wasn't really looking at her. He didn't see Eve any longer, only the Second.

She longed to hug her father, but that would shame him more than her in this moment. She still didn't accept all this, but he had.

"Goodbye, Papa," she whispered as she turned for the door. Her tears were spilling over.

Eve made her way back to her room and changed into a dress threaded with silver. It seemed far too precious for her to wear, but she bit her lip and pulled it on. The robe was not dissimilar to her uniform, just embroidered heavily. She walked to her classroom hoping she wasn't too late.

The Ernst seemed to have just begun. She saw, happily, that there was an empty seat for her.

"Please, excuse my tardiness," she asked her classmates and moved to her place, which was no longer at the back of the room. Many of the elite smiled at her as she took her seat.

"As I was saying," Ernst Peter continued as if nothing had changed, "if one throws a rock into the sea, does the rock become wet or does the sea become rocky?" He winked at her as she smirked.

"Is the rock porous?" she asked with the same smile. The class turned to her.

"Yes, very much so."

"Is this rock the only one in the sea?"

"I'm afraid so," he said with a sigh.

"Then the rock will become wet. And in time the sea will become rocky."

The Ernst looked to Eve's face, one white eyebrow raised.

"Eventually the rock will erode and coat the bottom of the sea in pebbles, making the sea rocky." And she dearly hoped she could. If she could leave enough pieces of herself behind, she might just make that big a change.

"Interesting," he mused. The class took a collective breath. None of them had ever made him pause like this.

The Ernst came to himself suddenly and continued with the class. "If a seed falls to the ground and no one witnesses it, does it still grow?"

Eve did not answer immediately, letting her peers draw their own answers. "Of course," one Vinca said. "If it fell on good soil, why wouldn't it grow?"

"How would you know that it did?" Eve asked. The Vinca turned to her, eyes wide. "Without a mind to witness, does it still have a purpose, does it still exist?"

The Ernst grinned widely at her with a twinkle in his eye. "And your answer, Most High?" he asked.

"Yes, it does. Because the seed has its own purpose, even without its own mind. It would exist to the insect that came to feed on its leaves. It would exist to the new plants growing from its seeds. I do not believe our world ceases to exist without us. It has its own purpose, and we are merely here to reap the benefits."

He closed his eyes and nodded. "But you are not sure," he asked her.

"Of course not. If I cease to exist tomorrow, I have no way of knowing that each of you will continue without me. But I believe that you do," she looked around the circle. Louis' jaw looked about ready to fall off.

"But enough of what I believe, what do you believe?" Eve asked, looking at the Ducati sitting beside her. "Do you believe the seed exists with no one to witness it?"

"I... I don't know."

"A valid answer," the Ernst told her. Eve smiled at her with encouragement. "These questions are not meant to be easy or obvious. Some of us spend more time contemplating them than others," he said grinning at Eve again. "If one is red and two is blue, what is three?"

Eve sighed and sat back, knowing her own answers to his questions, but enjoying learning those of her classmates.

As the class drew toward an end, Eve noticed Louis had fallen asleep, again. She leaned across the ring toward him. She snapped her fingers under his nose, eyeing him coolly while the rest of the class laughed at his startled expression. He rose, disgruntled, and left the room.

"Good riddance," the Ernst muttered. "Excellent, class. You are all progressing well. The aim is to reach your own answers, not simply agree with mine."

"Or hers," one of the Princes said, pointing at Eve who smiled and laughed.

"Or hers," the Ernst agreed.

Eve rose with the rest but did not hurry to the door. She came and kissed the Ernst's cheek. "Thank you, Honoured. You taught me much of myself. I am most grateful."

"I taught you nothing. You learned your own mind." He tapped a finger to his temple.

She bowed her head in agreement and bobbed a very small curtsy. He blushed deeply, and she laughed again.

"Are you tormenting Ernst Peter, Eve?" Adam asked from the doorway.

"I'm afraid so. Thank you again, Honoured." Eve touched his shoulder once more before moving to join Adam.

Adam held something in his hands. "You left something in the room," he said as he pinned her comb with bloom into her hair.

Eve smiled and blushed. "How could I have forgotten that?" she muttered to herself.

"Will you tell me who gave it to you? Do I need to worry about competition?"

She laughed loudly. "He found another while I attended here," she told him honestly. "His name is Lane. I can point him out to you at dinner."

"Best you don't. I might decide to be jealous." He held his hand for her to take.

She laughed again. "And why would you be jealous?"

Adam stopped short. He reached into his pocket and pulled out his favour. He placed it in her hand covering it with his own. Then he pulled his hand away to reveal the gift.

Eve gasped. It was so delicate. An opening flower bud formed out of copper.

"It is lovely!" she cooed, holding it up to see it more clearly. She pinned it to her dress between her breasts.

"The copper is pink enough?" Adam asked, still unsure of his favour.

"It is perfect," Eve assured him. "Thank you so much." She stood on tiptoe to kiss his cheek. "Is that the right response? The book wasn't that detailed." She giggled.

"Yes, that's appropriate." Adam smiled at her. "Now, I don't know about you, but I am ready for some lunch. I'm sure Mother is waiting for us, and she hates eating alone."

Lunch was taken in a room adjacent to Eve's new room. The High One, Mother, Eve reminded herself, was seated at a table. An older woman stood by a cart with several plates resting on it. The room was large with several chairs and two tables. Mother sat at one, and the other was covered in books.

"I'm sorry if we kept you waiting, mother," Eve apologized taking the seat on mother's right.

"You are sure you won't call me Bianca?" She asked again and then sighed. "Eve, this is Betty. She is our family Server."

"Betty," Eve said, acknowledging her. Then Eve sat back in her chair as Betty placed her meal before her.

"Eve," Mother asked now, "can you explain this cipher to me?" Eve noticed for the first time that her notes were at the table and Mother was reading them.

Eve turned her head to see the page. "Ah, yes. My second language is German, those are root abbreviations." She started to eat her lunch.

"Right, that makes sense now. I am receiving a report from Vinca Nancy. I think she might know some craftsmen to build your pots. May I present your ideas to her?"

Eve's eyes went wide. "Of course. I would appreciate that very much."

"Excellent, thank you." Eve blushed and looked into her plate. It was still odd being thanked by the Most High.

*

Adam stood next to Betty, behind the women. He hoped his mother would take pity on him and invite him to join them soon. He did enjoy watching Eve. It was obvious she was still adjusting to her new environs.

"Should I attend this meeting?" she asked, meeting Mother's green eyes. "I'm unsure how to spend my afternoons now. I'm unsure of almost everything!" Eve laughed.

"You could, or you could spend your afternoon in the library again. If you produce more writings like these," she tapped a page with her finger, "it will be easily as beneficial as attending with me."

Eve blushed again. "Perhaps there is someone who can instruct me on the specific duties of the Second. My classes were quite general. I know he counsels you on your decisions, fills in when you are ill or away, but what does that mean day to day?"

Adam smiled when his mother's eyes finally found him. "Oh, Adam. Please, sit with us."

Adam took the seat next to Eve, and she blushed. "We need to invite you to lunch?" she asked, her eyes wide.

"Yes."

"Well, I will remember to do so."

Betty brought Adam his lunch, and he began to eat. Moments later, he felt Eve's fingers on the back of his hand and nearly dropped his fork. She smiled shyly at him, gazing at him while he ate and trying to avert her eyes from time to time.

Bianca smiled, watching the little interplay. "Well, I'll let Adam instruct you on the duties of the Second. He seems the best choice. I will be off to meet Vinca Nancy. May I take these with me, Eve? There is a new one in your room if you need it." Bianca held the notebooks in her hands as she rose from her seat. Adam jumped to his feet and Eve rose as well.

"Please do. Thank you for a replacement. That second one is beginning to fill."

Mother nodded to them both and left the room. Eve sat and waited for Adam to do the same. She put her hand to his again, this time wrapping her fingers between his. "This is how servants show their affection for one another," she told him.

Her blush was divine. The colour in her cheeks made her glow. Adam wrapped a second hand around hers.

"An excellent method," he told her, bringing her fingertips to his mouth. "We don't usually show affection outside personal quarters, as you have learned."

"I had. Why is that?" she asked. She was quite curious.

"Where to begin?" Adam pondered. Her eyes were turning green. Putting a hand to her cheek, they became bluer again, and she looked away. He took the opportunity to gather his own thoughts. He brought his hand back to their joined ones.

"I suppose I should begin with our formal ties. As you know, many of our titles and honour are directly related to our bloodlines. What you don't know, is that blood is not always shared through the line." He flushed in embarrassment. "How to say this," he murmured looking down and seeing her favour. "This," he placed his hand over his favour, just over her heart, "is not related to marriage. Not really."

Her brow creased, and she muttered to herself, "But it talked of asking parents for permission. I'm sure I read..."

"If both parties are unwed, yes, they may do that, but more often, one or another family chooses a spouse, one which will gain the most honour for the family. This is very awkward to explain. Basically, who we are behind these doors, or more specifically those doors," he pointed to the bedroom doors, "need not, in any way, reflect who we are outside them. Does that make sense?"

*

Eve took several moments to digest what Adam had just told her. It sounded similar to servants seeking one another outside marriage, but marriages were involved here. Yet, these marriages, apparently, bore no similarity to those she knew. Her brow furrowed; she needed clarification.

"A little. So Richard?" Eve wasn't sure how to ask this.

Adam laughed. "He was my father, but I am not the rule. Perhaps the norm, though. Most of us do try to keep our families intact, but you knew Mother won him back from Aunt Victoria, right?"

Eve racked her brain; she couldn't recall any such history so she shook her head.

"Ah, well, Mother was in love with Richard and had planned to marry him, but Victoria got to Grandmother first. She and Richard were joined, and it strained family relations for a several years. Father still preferred Mother and so would meet with her. Eventually it became too difficult for Mother to bear seeing him with her sister so much of the time. Her only Cargon match was played, as ours, without witnesses versus Victoria. She won Richard for herself. Grandmother was furious with her. Richard was not as honoured as the husbands mother might have fetched, but Mother didn't care about that. Grandmother passed soon after. Then there were none left to question Mother's decision."

"So, when a man or woman is wagered..." Eve was trying to reconcile her previous beliefs with this new knowledge.

"Their bed always remains their own. Their quarters may not even move to a new part of the Palace, if they do not wish. Usually they do, though, it makes things easier. I noticed you had an incorrect assessment in your notes on that point."

"And no few nightmares," she admitted. Those horrible dreams of being passed from one man to another had been frightening and, apparently, completely unfounded. "Thank you for clearing this up for me. I was wondering what sort of society I had joined." She looked to their hands, still entwined. "But this is something beyond elite position?" she asked.

"Yes. This is much harder for us. There is a vulnerability to loving someone that elite do not relish. It is difficult to see the one you want on your hand sitting on the hand of another." He was taking his time searching for words. It seemed to Eve that he found this very hard to discuss with her.

"I think I understand enough for now." She tried to put him at ease. "Perhaps we can talk of duty instead?" she offered as Betty took their plates. "Just let me grab my notebook and a charcoal."

Adam didn't let go of her hand right away. She giggled a little as she pulled out of his grasp. Returning, she put charcoal to paper.

"I'm ready. Tell me all of my new service." She smiled.

"It's not a service, Eve," Adam reminded her.

"I know." She blushed. "It's just easier for me to think of it that way. I am a very special family Server," she said as she wrote a few notes about elite relations at the top of the page. "Please, tell me of my duty," she amended before he could ask her more.

After two hours of detailing his functions to her, Adam turned the tables. "Now tell me what you would have been doing, before you had access to library and classes anyway. What were your duties?"

"You really want to know?" she asked.

"Yes. I'm wondering what these are from." He rubbed his fingers over her few calluses.

"Well, in the mornings I would polish the silver service sets, unless I was mopping or cleaning tables. The afternoons were free, and you know what I did in the evenings."

"So what did you do on your free afternoons? We have some time before dinner. What would you like to do?" he asked, still stroking her hand. It was nice to be able to hold it.

Eve froze. She couldn't go to her friends, not like this. "Well, we would spend the time in the garden when the weather was nice."

"Excellent." He pulled her to her feet.

"No, Adam." She pulled her hands from his. "I can't."

"Why not?" he asked. "You can enjoy the garden."

"No," she pulled back again, feeling tears in her eyes. "I can't... I can't."

He touched her arm trying to calm her. "All right, not the garden. How about a quick walk through the quarters? I can show you the different wings; show you some of the reception halls?"

Eve took a deep breath to calm herself. "Yes, that would be lovely. Thank you." She took his arm gratefully and followed him out of the suite.

Adam stopped at one of the doors along the hall toward their suite. He knocked. "Aunt Maria? May we come in?" he asked.

"Adam?" a female voice answered.

"Adam!"

"Adam!" The pair of young voices was louder as they came through the door. They began chanting his name in unison.

Adam opened the door and was attacked by two black haired children. "James, Delilah, can you let us in?" he complained, shuffling his burdened legs. Eve followed, closing the door behind her.

The two children appeared to be ten or eleven, the boy a little older than the girl. They both had the same fair skin as Adam, though their hair was a little darker. They had green eyes, like their mother, Eve realized.

"You're the Server!" the boy exclaimed upon seeing her.

"The one Josephine tried to talk to," the girl shouted. Eve should have known they'd be in her decorum class, although she didn't recognize any faces from there, except the Ducati, Josephine's.

"You're very pretty," they said together.

"James! Delilah! Enough! You're behaving worse than Philip." The woman's voice was terse. "Welcome, Eve. We met last night. I'm Maria and these are your new siblings, I'm sorry to say." She looked at them with a hard expression.

The two pouted prettily. Adam put his lips to her ear, "Some new friends and family?"

She smiled and opened her arms to them. "James? Delilah? It is good to see you."

They took their cue and hugged her happily. "Where'd you get that bloom? Is it from one of our cousins?" James asked.

"You have two. That's because you're so pretty." Delilah added right on top of him.

"She's also very smart," an older girl said as she joined the group. Martina, if Eve remembered her name correctly. She'd been in labs with her and was in the class this morning.

"As smart as Adam?" Delilah wondered.

"No one's as smart as Adam," James complained.

Adam rolled his eyes. "You have to interrupt them," he informed her in a whisper. "They never stop." He continued in a louder voice, "Martina, you look lovely. How long until you join Uncle Albert and Aunt Maria at dinner?" He moved to stand beside her.

Eve didn't hear Martina's answer as the two started on her again. She held up her hands. "Wait!" she giggled. "Yes. I'm the Server, and, no, I'm not as smart as Adam, even though I did get the better of him once."

"Don't listen to her," Adam interrupted. "She's as smart as Mother."

Eve flushed as their two mouths hung open staring at her. "Hardly. This favour," she said by way of distraction, pulling her comb out of her hair. She gave it to Delilah, "is from a friend of mine. Another Server. And this," she pulled the copper pin from her breast and handed it to James, "is from Adam."

He flinched seeing the coming onslaught. "Adam?!"

"You really like her, Adam?" James asked.

"She's very pretty," Delilah murmured again.

"But she's our sister!" James objected.

"Yes, how does that work?" Delilah wondered now.

Eve moved to Maria's side, thankful for the release from their attention. "They stay with you?" she asked.

"Yes. The High One does not have much time for parenting. Adam she has kept with her since Richard's passing, but before he was here with us as well. James! Delilah! Get your dinner eaten! I want you both ready when Sally arrives to tutor you tonight." The children bounced quickly to the table at her tone. Adam now held both Eve's favours and brought them to her.

"Sally? Thank you." She pinned the bud on first with a smile.

"A Librarian." Adam was fixing the comb back in her hair.

Maria continued, "She brings them bedtime stories. I should be getting ready for dinner," she excused herself.

"As should we," Adam said, taking her arm.

Eve let go of him, approaching the table instead. She kissed one cheek of each of her new siblings. "I will visit again," she promised.

The post noon bell rang as they returned. "Should I visit the hair dresser still? Or does Betty see to us?"

"Betty tends to Mother. She should return shortly." Almost as if he had summoned her, Mother entered the suite behind them.

"Oh good, I haven't missed it. Come, Eve, we will dress you in something finer for dinner."

"Finer?" she murmured, barely able to imagine such.

Eve was led to a very large wardrobe in her new bedroom. Mother sat on the bed. Betty threw the doors open wide.

"Interesting. I don't think they will fit me though," Eve said in good humour, thumbing through Adam's jackets.

Mother clicked her tongue. "Henry assured me he would see to this," She grumbled. "Your new attire was to be moved in."

"And Adam's moved where?" Eve asked.

"That... was still to be determined."

Eve frowned. She suddenly liked this less and less. "I do not want to push him out of his own room."

"You earned his quarters, dear girl, and he knows it. If he was at all polite he wouldn't be listening at the door like some common vegetable grubber." She raised Her voice in his direction.

Eve giggled slightly as a sheepish Adam admitted himself. "Well, I am glad I will have the opportunity to change before dinner, at any rate. I'm sorry, I don't know where your things are, Eve."

She shrugged. "I'm happy in what I have on," she assured them both. They both shook their heads. Even Betty shook her head very slightly.

"Excuse me," Betty requested and ducked out.

"Well, maybe one of these will fit?" Eve teased, pulling out a jacket. "I can wear it over the dress?" She peeled off her robe and put her arms through before Adam could protest. "Perhaps not," she laughed looking at her fingertips barely reaching the bottom of the sleeves.

Mother roared with laughter. "Oh you are dear, child. I have not laughed so in months. However, I should go find my dress as Betty will be seeing to yours."

Eve shifted a little in the coat and then looked at Adam again. "Does it suit me?" she asked. "Could I start a new fashion?" She started to button it up.

He chuckled and grabbed her fingers. "I have no doubt you could, but the scandal!" he said, pulling the comb from her hair and tossing it on the bed. She followed it with her eyes and realized suddenly that they were alone in the room. She hunched a little in his jacket, letting it hide her blush. "You are too adorable," Adam chuckled.

The way he said it made her remember her father, and she felt tears spring to her eyes. She hadn't been able to touch him, to hug him. She would never be able to say goodbye. She was never to see her family again. Irrationally, she turned to the bed and grabbed the bloom from Lane, clutching it. One last reminder of who she had been, who she still was.

*

He must have offended her somehow; that was why she clutched her old favour. "I'll leave you," he said turning.

"Don't go," she shouted, grabbing for him. She put her head to his chest. "Please, don't go," she whispered, tears clouding her voice.

Her sorrow broke his heart. He quickly put his arms around her, squeezing very gently. "I won't go anywhere, unless you wish it," he murmured into her hair. "Can you tell me what is wrong?" He ran his hand through her hair, unsure if it was the right response.

She sighed. "I miss my family, my friends," she admitted. "You... you reminded me of my Pa. He would tell me I was adorable, his pretty." She sobbed more loudly. "He wouldn't say goodbye. He... he already saw me as Second. He didn't ... he won't ever..." She sniffed loudly and clutched him more tightly. "That's why I couldn't go to the garden. They... We can't..."

"I'm so sorry, Eve." He pushed her to sit on the bed, perching beside her. "I'm sorry this is hard for you."

She sniffed loudly again and tightened her lips. "I am with my family." He saw the beginning of more tears before she pulled his jacket up around her cheeks again.

Adam knelt in front of her, taking her hands. "You are. I am a poor substitute, but I will try to be all the family you could want. Even though we both know I can't succeed." He hung his head.

She put a hand to his cheek, pulling him to look at her again. "I can't do this without you. I wouldn't *be* doing this without you."

She looked at him intently now. Her eyes were blue again. What was she thinking now?

Eve traced the corner of his mouth with a finger where it turned down. She leaned forward and put her lips to his.

Adam's breath caught. He could taste her tears, still on her lips. He put a hand to her cheek, caressing it with his thumb.

Eve backed up very slightly and choked back the last of her tears. "I've wanted to do that for a while now," she admitted with a hysterical chuckle.

Adam rose slightly. He kissed her again, his hand trailing the back of her neck, pressing her hand to his chest with the other. He wanted her to know how much he wanted the same, how happy he was that she wanted him. How glad he was that they were able to be together.

He broke the kiss as he realized how much this had cost her. It was true that she had gained much, but right now her pain was paramount. "I'm sorry I have taken you from your family, but I am very glad to have you in mine."

She gripped his jacket and pulled him to her again. Her lips, her scent... He started to lean into her, taking more of her lips between his. His hands found her arms and pulled her more tightly to him, still leaning over her.

"Oh!" The squeak didn't come from Eve, but the woman behind them.

He closed his eyes and released Eve, backing up. "I'm sorry. I should not have pressed that far. It was wrong of me," he apologized to Eve.

Her eyes were still closed, and she lay on her back on the bed. She seemed to be almost panting. He wasn't even sure she'd heard his apology. He turned to Betty, who had placed Eve's evening attire on a chair in the corner. She was backing out of the room, discreetly.

"Adam?" Eve asked. "Do we need to attend dinner?"

"Yes, why?"

She sat up and started unbuttoning his jacket. "Because I think I'd like you to kiss me again."

"Eve," he pleaded, stopping her hand. "I think you don't want to make that choice right now. She looked up from her hands into his eyes again. Hers were an even lighter blue, pale. Adam could still see tears in them. She was definitely on an emotional edge. He kissed her gently. "Not that I don't want to take you up on that offer," he whispered.

She giggled a little. “But you’re not sure I’m in my right mind?” she asked. Taking a deep breath, she stood up. “You are right that I am not.” She walked to the dress on the chair. It was golden yellow in colour, and she held it up to herself.

“That colour suits you,” Adam told her. It gave her pale skin a pearly glow. It set off her eyes, whether blue or green. “I’ll go and let you change,” he said as he rose. “I’ll just take this with me.” He took his jacket from her shoulders.

She blushed again, letting it go.

Mother came out while Adam was between jackets. “Is that the one Eve had on?” she asked as he pulled it on. He smiled sheepishly and looked at his boots. “I see,” she said with a smirk. She saw too much, as always. “I was thinking that there is a closet over there that would have enough room for a bed. If you don’t want to find new quarters,”

Adam looked up with hope. He really didn’t want to abandon Eve here even for the night. A closet, he thought, had he really sunk so low? Yes he had.

“Thank you, Mother.”

She straightened his collar. “What you men won’t do for women,” she muttered.

*

Eve stepped out of the room. The robe, as it turned out, was black, contrasting with both her skin and her dress. She did not understand how they had things in her size, but pinned the copper bud back in place between her breasts, regardless. The fabric bloom from Lane was safely tucked in a pocket.

“Is Betty ready for my hair? It is a challenge, just to warn her.”

“I think I can handle it, Most High,” she said confidently, pulling out a chair.

Eve settled in it, lifting her hair over the back. Betty, in addition to styling Eve’s hair, applied cosmetics. Eve hoped no one expected her to be able to paint herself the way Betty did. A looking glass was placed in Eve’s hand once Betty finished. Had she not held it herself, Eve would not have believed she was the woman in the reflection. Her hair was not piled as she normally wore it, but instead, half was looped up through a silver band on her head and the rest spilled down her back.

"You are an artist," Eve admired Betty's work. "Well, I suppose I'm properly attired now?"

Adam gasped when she rose and turned. "It's not possible," he whispered.

Eve looked over her shoulder. Did he see a ghost? What wasn't possible? That she was standing in this room, in these clothes?

"All right," Mother taunted, nudging him into movement. "You've gawked. Now let's go; we're late."

Adam kept Eve on his arm all the way to the dining hall. Several times she looked to him for courage along their walk. She had entered the hall through the main doors on occasion before, but never while the elite were seated. She was reminded again how completely her world had been turned on its head.

It was only when she looked down and saw her dress and new slippers that she remembered she wasn't in her uniform. She had already forgotten her face paint.

They followed the High One to Her seat, and Adam held Eve's chair as she sat. Then he turned to find his own seat.

Eve grabbed for him as he started to leave. "You aren't sitting with us?" She didn't want him to go; he was her strength, her courage.

Adam looked to his mother, and they both looked at Eve. "My place is no longer here," he informed her. "I'll be just over there, at that end of the table." He pointed for her. "Not far."

Her eyes were still wide and she bit her lip briefly. Mother patted her hand where she clutched Adam's arm, and Eve let go. Mother smiled and took her hand, patting it again.

"It will be fine," she assured Eve.

Eve took the opportunity to taste the wine she so often poured. She sipped the white very carefully, unsure what her reaction would be. It was dry and puckered her lips, but tasted very nice.

"So, he is the least of the Vanto now?" Eve asked, looking to Adam at the end of his table.

Mother nodded, starting on her next course. "He might be higher if there were a portfolio open for him, but sadly, there isn't."

Eve motioned the Server for the red; she wanted to sample both. Never having had either, she didn't know her preference. Mother noticed.

"This is the first time you've had wine, isn't it?"

"Yes." The red was much sweeter. She wasn't sure yet, but she believed she liked it better.

"Try not to exceed the two cups," she warned. "It will hit you harder the first time."

Hit her? The alcohol? She had seen some elite stagger from the hall, influenced by the wine. Making a note to pace herself, she made sure the white was not even half empty yet.

"Vinca Nancy was pleased to hear of your improvements to kitchen implements. She is passing the information along."

"That's wonderful!" Eve said with a smile and clapping her hands. She giggled and Mother joined her. "Too much?" she asked.

"No, it is good to enjoy your work."

"Mother, who else would be acceptable to sit with us? When you wed Richard, before your mother passed, did he?"

"Planning your marriage already?" Mother smirked.

Eve blushed more brightly.

The last of the elite were leaving when Eve rose with her new mother. She swayed and sat back in her chair with a thump. The room spun slightly.

Mother chuckled, "I'm going to see to the board. I'll be back."

Eve tried to stand again and made it to her feet this time though the room still seemed unsteady around her. Was it the wine? She was glad she hadn't had more, planning to only have one cup next time. Mother was nearly finished when Eve had made her tentative way to the board.

"Better yet?" Mother asked.

"A little," Eve admitted. "I'd feel better with your hand for the walk back, if I may?"

Mother smiled broadly, "Of course! I'm surprised that son of mine didn't stay to escort you himself."

"He wanted to check his bed was prepared before he intruded on your suite again." Adam caught Eve's elbow as she spun to face him. He laughed. "Too much wine?" Her face was a little flushed, but aside from the wobble she felt well enough.

"Just a tad," she giggled. "My new limit will be one total instead of one of each," she vowed.

"Very wise," Mother said sagely. She turned to Adam, "I presume your bed is in place then?"

"Yes. I shall have to beg Eve for space in her wardrobe however."

Eve was a little confused but couldn't see any problem with this. "Certainly, but speaking of bed, I think I should like to be in mine, before I do or say something too foolish."

"Oh come, Eve." Mother patted her hand and held it while Adam tucked the other through his arm. "You've done and said nothing foolish."

"Precisely," Eve pointed out. She hiccupped and turned a brighter red.

Their chuckling was very quiet as they supported her between them.

CHAPTER FIVE

Eve awoke on the most comfortable bed, from the deepest sleep. Her mouth felt terrible, like it was filled with fuzz. She rinsed it quickly with water from her wash pitcher and then wet her face. That was when she saw for the first time where she was.

The room was opulent; the bed had a multi-hued canopy and beautifully carved and polished posts, the floor was covered in carpets. She looked down at herself and was surprised at the elegance of her night dress. It was going to take many mornings before she could begin her day without gazing in wonder.

She opened her door and peeked out. Mother was in her night dress at a table, Betty standing behind her. She was sipping her morning tea and waved Eve out.

"Good morning! Did you sleep well? No after effects of the wine, I hope?"

Eve smiled. She would never have guessed how friendly the High One would be when she was a Server, but it was almost as though she had found a long-lost aunt in this second mother. "Yes and no." She sat across from Mother and Betty set a plate with fried eggs before her. Usually her breakfasts were cold.

There was a yawn behind her, and Eve looked over her shoulder. Adam came out with his hair rumpled, a little stubble on his chin, and only pants on. Eve blushed and looked back at her eggs.

He didn't take a seat but moved to Betty, pouring himself a cup of tea while he waited. Eve glanced up enough to see Mother grinning at her.

"Adam, would you join us?" Eve asked in a voice that nearly squeaked.

"I would, thank you," he smiled at her, running a hand through his hair again. This drew more attention to his chest, at which Eve was trying very hard not to stare. She decided to pour herself a cup of tea as a distraction. She slopped twice before hitting the cup. Mother chuckled.

"Are you sure you want me here?" he asked now, steadying her hand.

Eve set the pot down, closed her eyes and took a breath. "I'm sure I don't want you to go," she relented.

Mother laughed out loud. "I could have told him that!"

"Don't tease her," Adam hissed. "I'll go get a shirt."

Mother saw her momentary frown and laughed again. "Not exactly what you want?" She asked amidst chuckles. Eve flushed again, slinking down in her chair.

"Ignore her," Adam whispered into Eve's ear, sending a shiver down her spine.

"You really need a bell or something," she complained.

They both looked at her quizzically. "You keep sneaking up on me!"

They both laughed now, and the family resemblance shone. Their faces were very similar, although their colouring differed slightly. Adam's skin a little ruddier and his hair lighter than his mother's milk-white complexion and black hair. Eve sipped her tea as she straightened in her chair. "What are we doing today?" she asked.

"Well, I have another meeting this morning with Vanto Albert and Vinca Della. They didn't finish before noon yesterday, but you needn't come to that. Adam can sit in for you," Mother replied.

"I want to come. I want to fulfill my duties." Eve sat up straighter. She was sure she could do this.

*

Adam watched her change. She went from the small girl with the blue eyes and wonderful blush, to the woman with fierce green eyes and determination in her chin. He couldn't decide which he admired more. Was it possible he could win both for himself?

Eve noticed him staring at her. She smiled at him and took his hand. "I'm real, you know. Not a ghost. You were looking at me like that last night, too."

"You can't be real. Any minute now Ernst Peter is going to come in and ask me some nonsense about the light failing in the sky."

Eve laughed merrily. "Ah, yes. If all the stars fell from the sky, would night end or continue forever?" she quoted. "Well, unless the sun is a star, morning would come regardless," she laughed with her own answer.

How readily she answered! He had never been able to form words to his own ideas surrounding these questions. The sun as a star? "Do you think the sun might be a star?" he asked now.

"Hmm, I hadn't considered it that much. It would depend on the relative movements of the bodies, I suppose. If the light of the sun were far enough from us, it might appear the same as the stars. I have not studied that subject, not being free to stargaze," she said with a smirk.

She hadn't... and yet.... Her mind was amazing.

"Close your mouth, dear," his mother told him snidely.

Eve giggled again. At least she was amused.

"Will you help me choose my attire?" she asked Mother. "Or Betty?"

"Well, Adam needs to use your wardrobe, anyway. I'm sure he can choose something appropriate. If he can't, we won't let him dress himself," Bianca teased.

It was worth being teased to amuse Eve, not simply to be ribbed.

*

Adam rolled his eyes and rose from his empty plate. When had he eaten it all? Eve hadn't even noticed him lift a fork. She still had most of an egg left, but she didn't want to linger. Betty followed Mother to her room and Eve followed Adam to hers. She watched his stride, his bare feet. Was that how he was so quiet all the time? She tried to imitate him.

Adam opened the wardrobe. "Let's see."

Eve stepped up beside him. She looked at the jackets on the left half and thumbed through a few. A blue one, which she singled out, would look especially good with his eyes.

"I think that is probably more of an evening jacket," he whispered in her ear with another chuckle.

She laughed, too. "Really? Because I was sure I could wear it to the library today. It seems the perfect reading jacket to me." She held it up to herself.

Adam laughed again and shook his head. He pulled it from her and hung it back up, then pulled out a white dress with pearls on the sleeves. She couldn't imagine sewing such things into clothing, but she was learning to imagine a lot of new things. He held this up to her, then put it into her hands and flipped through the robes. The one he chose was a light rose.

"Oh, no," she protested, "that is far too lush."

He smiled. "Yes. Feel it. This is my favourite fabric. Our neighbours have a type of rabbit with hair of this." He lifted the robe to her cheek, and she closed her eyes at the feathery touch.

He kissed her again while her eyes were still closed. "You like it?" he asked.

"Yes," she answered and kissed him again. He pulled back a little. "Oh, you meant the robe? Yes, it's very nice."

He blushed. "Well, I'll just grab my things." He rummaged a little longer, coming out with matching dark grey pants and jacket. Eve watched him go.

She stepped out to find Mother sitting with her tea while Betty tended her hair. Eve sat in the chair Adam had occupied previously. She set one foot on the empty chair, watching Betty work.

She jumped a little when she felt a hand on her ankle.

"May I?" Adam asked.

"Please," she said, sitting up and pulling her leg back. He didn't let go, instead setting it on his knee. He rubbed her toes absently while pouring himself another cup.

She gasped at one point when he hit a ticklish toe and twitched her foot.

"Hmm, tender?" he asked. Betty had just come to stand behind Eve. Adam put both his hands to her foot now, and Eve moaned a little as the touch worked out long held knots, especially when Betty's gentle manipulations of her hair had her scalp tingling, too. She closed her eyes and leaned her head back with a sigh.

Mother chuckled. "Don't fall asleep now. You'll miss all the fun."

Eve opened her eyes again. Adam was still stroking the top of her foot while his chin was tipped up. He was lathered with some sort of cream, and Betty held a knife to his throat. Eve gasped.

"Never seen a man shaved before?" Mother asked. "It looks dangerous, doesn't it?"

"Does it hurt?" Eve had to ask.

Adam waited until the next time Betty was wiping her blade. "Only when she nicks me."

"I have not nicked you in months, Most High," Betty said in a light scoff.

"And it hasn't hurt in months," he said with a smile. "I try not to tease her when she's holding the knife."

"Wise," Eve murmured, pulling her foot back and rising to watch more closely. The blade was scraping along the skin, taking the hair along with the cream. She wondered if there wasn't a better way to do this – safer, gentler. She would have to think on it. She'd never really considered facial hair at all before. When Betty was done, she ran a finger down his cheek.

"Smooth?" he asked. "Or should I have her do it again?" His eyes twinkled at her.

She put her lips to his cheek now. "Very smooth," she whispered.

He sighed at the lightness of her touch. Mother was chuckling again. "You two are going to have me looking for someone new if you keep that up. However, we should be going. Vanto Albert and Vinca Della will be waiting on us otherwise." Mother took one last sip of tea and set Her cup down.

Betty handed Eve her slippers, and she pulled them on quickly. Adam found and tugged on his boots. Eve noticed his room briefly. He wasn't really sleeping in a closet, was he? She shook her head as the door closed again quickly. She must have imagined it was as small as that.

Eve walked beside Adam to the meeting room. There was a raised platform at one end where the High One sat and two small tables to either side. An Ernst sat at one and Adam led her to the other. There was only one chair and he motioned for her to sit in it.

"But what about you?" she asked, looking over her shoulder.

"I will stand right here. If you have any questions, just ask. If you have any suggestions, tell Mother. If you feel you aren't ready for this, just say so. You don't need to do this today."

That sounded like a challenge. She straightened and faced the door through which Vanto Albert and Vinca Della would enter. Adam nudged a piece of paper to her.

"That's the last meeting's transcript. If there's anything you don't understand, I can fill you in." Of course, he had been here yesterday morning while she was in class.

They had updated the High One on various neighbours, but had run long when it came to Augustia to the south. They were now discussing an internal conflict and how it was expected to affect trade. Eve tried to dredge up her memories of Augustia and what trade was likely there. Some points were listed on the page, and she was able to find her notes, which mentioned some others.

She picked up a charcoal from the desk and started writing notes at a furious pace; she'd missed so much in the minutes it had taken her to get caught up. Adam nudged an ink pot toward her.

"There is a pen."

"This is faster," she whispered, focusing on the discussion. All attention seemed to be on the result of the ensuing conflict. Wasn't it neighbourly to help diffuse this situation, if possible? It didn't seem to have been considered at all.

Adam looked over her shoulder. "Vanto Albert?" he asked. "The Second has a question for you."

Eve looked up at him, eyes wide. He tipped his head to the Vanto, urging her to speak.

"Um, yes. I was wondering what might be causing this strife. Might there not be some way to mitigate it before trade is compromised? Do we know what the conflict is?"

"Not really," Vanto Albert answered. "We know the conflict lies between the common class and the elite; but beyond that, we do not have much detail. Obviously, though, if the common class revolts, there will be no goods for trade."

Eve took a deep breath. "Unless the common folk were to conduct the trade." It was as though black powder had gone off and everyone stood silent in the quiet after the explosion.

"Common... trade?" Della asked. "The commoners do not know how to conduct trade."

"Do they not?" Eve asked. "I think exchanging one good for another is fairly easily understood. Even the servants conduct such exchanges, although perhaps they are *simpler* than trade. If we were to simplify our process, we might be able to continue to provide our neighbours with the goods they require while disrupting ourselves as little as possible."

The High One smiled at Eve and nodded to her once.

The Vanto and Vinca looked at each other, then at the High One, and then at Eve. "We... have not considered the possibility, Most High. We will need time to... simplify the process. We must also consider any problems this may cause in dealing with the elite or even the possibility that it might undermine their efforts to restore their balance."

"Of course. I was only making a suggestion. Another?" She paused to see if anyone would interrupt her. "It might be beneficial to understand this conflict better. It would certainly aid in choosing our approach in the future."

"Yes, Most High," Albert agreed immediately. "I shall endeavour to determine that on my next visit. In the meantime, I would suggest meeting with Ducat Clarence. He is currently assigned to Augustia. You may be able to make more of his information than I."

Eve blushed immediately. "I would not presume," she murmured, bowing her head. Adam touched her neck, stroking downward. She should not demure herself this way and lifted her chin. "An excellent suggestion, Vanto. If the High One agrees?" Eve looked to Mother now.

Bianca nodded. "It is a good idea, and you will most definitely be present at that session, Eve." The High One smiled broadly, proud of her protégé. "In the meantime, tell us more about how you think we might be able to work around these trade concerns you have raised, Vinca."

Eve resumed taking notes, her charcoal flying to keep up with Della's report.

"You know that the Ernst is transcribing this entire meeting. You'll be able to read the whole thing," Adam whispered to her now.

"Yes, that will be most helpful." She continued to scribble. "I'm not simply writing what she's saying - I'm adding my interpretation, what it means beyond the words. For instance, if we are unable to get salt from Augustia, is there a substitute rather than simply another source? I happen to know there is. I can make salt from minerals found locally. It is not as fine as what we can get from Augustia, however. If our supply of oil is limited in future, we might choose to ration what we have." She tried to focus on the Vinca's report again.

*

Adam was stunned. She could glean all that from this simple report? She could make salt? How did she do that? He wanted to ask, but she was listening so carefully that he didn't want to interrupt again. She was magnificent; what a waste it had been for her to simply pour wine.

Adam looked at his mother now, and she met his eye, winking at him. His mother knew what she had found. He didn't doubt she'd been watching for one such as Eve. In fact, as he thought on it, he knew she had. She had chosen the last three Librarians in this manner. Mother hadn't expected Eve to go as far as she did, initiating the match, but she had been prepared to put her into greater service if she hadn't.

He felt decidedly dense surrounded by these brilliant women. He stepped back and watched them work for a while.

The High One looked to Eve as the report drew to a close. Eve nodded to her.

"Thank you, Albert, Della. We will await your next report, and please send Ducat Clarence to Ernst Alexander, here, so we might make an appointment to meet with him." The High One dismissed them. "That went very well. You will be an excellent Second, Eve." Mother rose from her seat. "I must say, I wasn't expecting to find you in quite this position, but I cannot regret that you are." Eve blinked as Mother leaned over the table. She turned the new notebook around and read over the page.

"You should learn the Ernst's shorthand. Although your cipher is very clever, his serves him very well. Honoured Alexander? Would you show us your notes?"

Alexander brought his pages to the desk and placed them before Mother and Eve. Eve turned them to read better. Between these and the transcript from yesterday, Eve could quickly make out what the symbols that looked like strange letters meant. "Yes, I see. Thank you, Honoured." She quickly jotted down a key with these symbols for future use.

Mother clucked her tongue disapprovingly. "You really should use the pen. Look at your fingers."

Eve blushed and pulled her hand into her sleeve. "It washes," she insisted. "I'm not nearly as quick with a pen," she admitted, "and much sloppier. I prefer the charcoal."

"Then perhaps we shall have to find you some gloves, or a holder," Adam suggested, taking her hand. He longed to kiss it, but that would be too much. It was still a thrill to have her so near, so often, to be able to touch her.

"Mother?" Eve asked. "Could we have a second chair for the Vanto?"

"I'm afraid he can't stay long, Eve. I can have only one Second," Mother said, looking down. "You are fitting in much more quickly than I could have dreamed. I shall have to find a new place for him sooner than I thought." She met his eyes, regret filling hers.

It wasn't her responsibility to find a place for him. He would have to make his own way as any other of the elite did, working their way toward a portfolio, or finding a niche that hadn't been filled.

Eve's face crumpled. "There must be some way. If he were mine? Not my Second, obviously, but... my husband?" she suggested. She looked from one to another.

Adam wasn't sure he'd heard her correctly. She couldn't really be suggesting that, not so soon.

"That could work," Mother admitted, and Adam's eyes flew to her.

"Mother, you can't honestly be suggesting she settle for a husband with so little honour as I have now." It was ludicrous.

"You would talk to me about husbands of insufficient honour? I think I wrote the book on that. Also, I'm not suggesting it, she is. He is right, however. It would mean relinquishing your chance to take a more honourable husband. You might want to think on this, Eve. You needn't decide immediately. I won't lose Adam until I'm sure you're ready for your new role. If this is what you want, though, I don't see a reason why you couldn't marry him."

She nodded. "I will contemplate, and I will learn. I still do not understand why honour is so important in marriage, but if you will both be so kind as to teach me, I would be grateful. There is much that is not written," she said with a smile. "For instance, no book will tell you that several servants maintain nooks for quiet moments alone. Is it this way with the elite?"

Adam flushed crimson. Was she asking how they trysted?

Mother laughed. "Not quite the same, no. We can each use our own rooms, thankfully. The benefit of not sharing quarters." Adam felt even worse; his mother was discussing this? With the girl whose favour he sought? Did she not see his favour on Eve?

"Adam?" she asked. "Are you quite well?"

"Yes, Mother. I'm fine." He thought he would appreciate the floor swallowing him right now.

Eve turned to look at him, and he turned a brighter shade of red. "You are sure?" she asked, rising and putting a hand to his head.

"Yes, yes. Please, both of you, don't fuss." He took her hands to keep her from noticing how quick his heart was thumping at the moment.

"He just needs some lunch," Mother suggested.

"And this afternoon?" Eve asked.

"Another meeting. This one will be with Prince Carlton regarding the state of our mounts. He is worried that the elite are not riding their horses enough," she said with a laugh. "You needn't attend if you'd rather be about other things."

"Actually, I'm quite interested in horses. My father serves in the stable, so I've seen them quite often. I'd like to attend."

"Then, by all means, my dear."

Adam opened the door for them at the suite. "I think I'll visit Ernst Derek. I want to see if he can show me how to *make* salt."

"Oh, yes," Eve stammered, blushing and looking down.

"Make salt?" Mother mused. "Why would he know that? How would he do that? Oh, sit down, Adam." Bianca shook her head, though he was grateful for even the short invitation.

"Eve?" Adam asked with a smile.

She closed her eyes for a moment after taking her seat. "A saturated solution can form crystals," she said taking a seat for lunch. "If you dissolve the proper minerals into solution you can form salt crystals in this manner. It so happens that limestone, properly crushed, can do this very well in simple acids. Like vinegar." She stopped to eat a bite of her lunch. "However, vinegar will not make a true salt. You need the proper acid for that. Stomach acid, I believe. Hmm, distasteful discussion for lunch," she complained as she took another bite.

They were both still staring at her. "What?" Adam asked.

Her eyes were like emeralds now, utterly confident. She had never worked the magic she described, Adam was certain, but she knew without a doubt that it could be done. Her hold to logic was impenetrable and flawless, that he could see.

"How would you saturate the solution?" he asked.

"Distilling, simple boiling. Acids with bases make water. Remove the water." She took a sip of tea, as though this was all most obvious, and to her it was.

"Well, Eve, that is... a solution to our salt problem should it arise. We can get stomach acid from the pork immediately after slaughter. I imagine this wouldn't yield a significant quantity of salt?"

"No. It is certainly a much better idea to import naturally formed salt. It is of higher quality. Also, this process is quite time consuming. If we find we are in need of a temporary supply, it could suffice."

"Very good. I will see to it that Vinca Nancy knows of this in the event that salt does become an issue. Adam? Are you still planning to spend the afternoon with Ernst Derek in the lab?"

"I... I think I shall. I think I need a refresher science course."

Eve chuckled, "I imagine I have been in class more recently than you."

*

He squeezed her hand before rising. Again, he'd managed to inhale his meal while she wasn't looking. She was usually a very fast eater, grabbing lunch enroute from class to the library, but Adam, she was sure, didn't chew at all.

"You are quite right, of course. I'll meet you here before dinner," he told both ladies while heading out the door.

Betty was adjusting Eve's hair while she sipped her tea. She pulled out her bloom and passed it to Betty. "Since he isn't going to be there. It matches the robe so well," she told Mother.

"Only because he's not," She said with a smile.

"Did I embarrass him by talking of love making?" she asked.

"Oh, yes, right out of his wits." Mother laughed. "He can be so prudish sometimes."

"So, do you?" Eve asked arching her eyebrow while sipping her tea.

"Not in a long while," Mother said with a small sigh. "I consider it from time to time, but so few are interesting beyond the first few moments. I really was spoiled by Richard. He was a friend and a lover. I find I want nothing less now."

Eve nodded. That made perfect sense. "Are you meeting Prince Carlton at the stables? Should I find shoes?" She hoped not.

"Yes, we were going to ride a little around the grounds, for the exercise. You would join us?"

Eve's mouth fell open. She'd patted the horses, fed them, but she'd never ridden one. "Would I need anything?"

"Oh, you would need to change gowns. You'll need one divided for riding." Mother led her to the wardrobe and pulled one out. "I'll wait for you," She said, closing the door behind Her.

Eve followed behind Mother, hoping that her father would not be attending them. She wasn't ready to face him again yet, especially without Adam at her side.

"Good day, Most High," Prince Carlton greeted them.

"Good day, Highness," Eve and the High One both greeted him. Eve watched the Prince and Mother mount their horses. Then she saw her father leading out a third mount for herself. They hadn't expected her, of course.

"And what is this lovely lady's name?" Eve asked her father without looking at him. She patted the mare's nose and tried not to let her voice shake.

"Bella, Most High," he answered.

"A beautiful name for a beautiful creature," she murmured. She took a deep breath and moved to the stirrup, putting her left foot in as she had seen the other two do.

"May I, Most High?" her father asked, offering to help with her other leg.

"Thank you, Pa," she whispered. He looked up very briefly and she beamed at him, tears brimming her eyes. "This is my first ride," she said unnecessarily. "It is all very new and a little frightening."

"Well, Bella, here, is as tame as they come. She'll give you no trouble. You needn't fear, Most High," her father assured her. "You seem very adaptable. I'm sure you'll have the knack in no time."

"I do hope you are right." It was very hard not to thank him, but she was sure he would react as poorly as she had to Adam only a week ago. Instead, she clucked to Bella as she'd seen her father do to coax the horse into moving. She fell in behind the Prince and Mother easily.

Eve sat in a tub beside Mother after their ride. "This is marvelous," she murmured, sinking in the warm water. "We usually just sponge down. I don't think I've been immersed in water since I went to the pond when I was six."

"A luxury, for certain. The water goes to the garden after, so at least it isn't a complete waste. Still," Mother sighed, "if I had to waste water on something, I don't know that I could think of a better way."

"How often do you do this?" Eve asked, raising her legs from the water to cool her skin and sink her torso a little lower.

"At least once a week, if I can fit it in."

"Do the other elite take turns in this same room?" she asked, looking at the other empty tubs. "Prince Carlton for instance."

"He would probably be here if he weren't still in the stable," she said in agreement. "It must be a busy afternoon for everyone else. Well, I have started to wrinkle. I'm getting out."

Eve wondered at that. She was wrinkling? Eve looked at her hands and noticed the creases in the tips. Oh, of course, wrinkling. She stood in the tub and grabbed her towel from the stand. She put her eyes down as two other elite entered.

"I take it we are all equal in this room?" Eve asked Mother as she dried off. The two men were undressing behind them.

"That's right. One of the few. We don't usually linger in this room though, not outside the tub." They both dressed quickly and returned to the suite to prepare for dinner. Betty took the extra time as an opportunity to wash Eve's hair, something that she hadn't had done in over a week. It was harder and harder to find that kind of time with the hair dressers. She didn't go more often than was necessary.

She had her head in the basin when Adam came in from his afternoon in the lab. "Make good salt?" she asked.

"No, broke some glass beakers, though," he said with a smile.

She wrinkled her nose. She would have never guessed he was one of *those* boys. "You overheated it," she accused.

"Actually, no," he said, taking off his jacket and going to her room to hang it. He came out with the blue one she had picked that morning. "The process was too quick - it expanded in the jar."

"You need to change shirts," Eve informed him. "You smell like vinegar."

He sniffed and Mother laughed. He went back into Eve's room. Betty wrapped Eve's hair in a towel and went to tend Bianca's hair. Eve came in while Adam was between shirts. "Excuse me," she said, stopping at the door.

He pulled it on and turned. "Not a problem. What are you going to wear tonight?" he asked.

"I have no idea. I still don't really know what I have," she admitted, stepping up to the wardrobe. She flipped through several dresses, not really knowing which were for day wear and which for evening.

Adam's arm reached over hers, reminding her of their match in the dining hall. She smiled and stepped back very slightly. She could now, and it was so nice to be free to do so.

He chuckled and put his lips to her ear, pulling his arm back and wrapping it around her waist. He put the other to her hip, as well. His sigh sent shivers through her.

"You really think I should consider honour over this?" she asked, leaning her head into his. She turned to let her nose, and then her lips, trace his jaw line.

He sighed again. "This doesn't have to be a marriage," he reminded her.

She dropped her head and stepped out of his arms. Unable to articulate it, she would always equate the two. They were not separable for her as they were for him.

*

Adam cursed himself. What a stupid thing to say. Would anything make him happier than marrying her? It would be excellent for him in terms of standing, as well, but terrible for her.

"I'm sorry," he apologized readily.

"You don't need to apologize. It's the way you were raised. Love and marriage are not associated in your world as they are in mine. Well, the world I was raised in." She pulled out a deep blue dress. "How about this one?" she asked, turning to face him.

"That will do nicely. Eve, I-"

She held up a hand. "Everything is fine, Adam, really." To prove it, she stepped forward and kissed him again, lightly. His hand came up to brush her cheek with his fingers. Her skin was so soft. She smelled of the baths, the perfume they added to the water.

He pulled the towel from her head, letting her still dark damp hair down. It released more of her scent with it. She shivered a little as her dress became wet.

He searched every tiny segment of her face, wanting to memorize every line, every curve. He wanted to kiss every one of them. She started to flush under his scrutiny.

"My eye is out of line," she said quietly.

"What?" he asked, blinking and settling back on her deep blue eyes.

"You were looking for a flaw. I have one eye out of line."

He laughed and hugged her to himself. "I wasn't looking for a flaw." He kissed the top of her head. Holding both her cheeks, he looked into her face again. "Well, so it is."

She closed her eyes and laughed.

"It's just as well you sent me back. I need a new pair of pants for this jacket." He pulled them out, they were scarlet.

Eve quickly changed into the blue dress and found a silvery robe to wear over it. She came out as Adam stepped out of the door to his closet.

"You aren't sleeping in here, are you?" The closet was barely big enough for the cot crammed into it.

Adam laughed. "I think they may have actually found me your old bed," he joked.

She took another look at it. "No, I'm pretty sure my mattress was thicker."

Mother laughed loudly.

Adam narrowed his eyes in his mother's direction. "Well, it will suffice for now." He closed the door deliberately.

"Are they preparing you new quarters?" Eve asked.

"Yes, Adam, are they?" Mother asked with a glitter in her eyes. She lived to torment him. Surely she chose to have children just for moments like these.

"No, not yet. I wanted to be around for your first days. In case you needed a friend who didn't torment you." He looked meaningfully at his mother. She only laughed again.

"Does she always laugh this much?" Eve asked in a whisper. "I don't remember that from dinner."

Adam shook his head with a smile playing on his lips. Although he was irritated with her this moment, it was nice to see his mother so happy. Perhaps a new daughter was reawakening the child in her?

"Well, I do appreciate that, Adam, but you should not trust your sleep to that cot for long. My bed is more than large enough for two."

Adam spluttered and Mother roared again, clapping her hands this time. "And you didn't hear last night!" she said between peals. "Too good, you are too good, child."

Eve's mouth fell open and she clicked it shut. She blushed and shook her head, putting a hand to her face. "Servers often share beds. Not often with the opposite sex, to be sure, but it has been done. I didn't mean to imply..."

"Of course you didn't." Mother was still laughing. "That's what makes it so funny!"

Mother was having entirely too much fun at their expense. "Don't you need to be getting dressed?" Adam asked snidely.

"You watch your tongue, Vanto," she said with another chuckle. "If you want time alone, you should ask nicely." She laughed more loudly at her own joke. "Oh, come with me, Betty; they don't appreciate my humour anyway."

As Betty followed Bianca, it was obvious from the set of her mouth that she was fighting laughter of her own. Once the door closed, a new peal was heard.

"Honestly," Adam muttered. "Don't mind her. She just wants to make you comfortable and me uncomfortable, I think. She seems to not mind your discomfort too much either, actually."

"Well, I mind your discomfort." She looked to the closet again. "What we do in there is independent of anything outside, right?" she verified, looking to her door now.

"Yes," he said a little shakily. Did she really want that?

"Then, if we sleep on opposite sides, no one would know one way or the other, would they?" she asked.

She was too smart, and too generous, and too trusting! "I... I will think on it. Not tonight."

She smiled broadly. "I expect your back will make your decision for you." She took a seat so Betty might set her hair when she returned with Mother.

CHAPTER SIX

Eve woke, washed her face and wondered if she was in the right room. Where was Sarah? She blinked the water from her eyes and memory returned. Two weeks hadn't made her accustomed to her environs. This was her room — hers alone, ridiculously. It was huge. A small family could share it. She yawned and went to greet Mother.

"Mo-orning," she said around another yawn.

"Good morning, Eve," Mother greeted her. Betty poured Eve's tea.

"What is planned for today?" Eve asked as her breakfast was served.

"Actually, I'm going out of the palace overnight."

Eve froze with her fork on the way to her mouth. She spent a second thinking and then finished the bite. "Adam is staying," she verified.

Mother grinned. "Yes. If you have any troubles, he'll be here to help you handle them. You won't need him though. It's just an overnight excursion. I'll be back for dinner tomorrow. You will tend the board?"

"Of course," Eve agreed readily. That task was one she enjoyed and felt confident undertaking. "There is nothing else that needs to be seen to?"

"No. These days are yours. Enjoy it. I'm sure we'll be working you hard in the days to come. This trip was planned before you began your challenge. I'd considered moving it, but I have no concerns. You will heed Adam's advice or shun it if you have a better plan of your own. As I said, nothing will come up. It's only one day. I must be off early, though. That is no doubt why that lie-a-bed son of mine isn't up yet!" She raised Her voice and threw Her slipper at his door.

An unintelligible mumble came from inside.

"Well, take care of the boy. I'm sure he will need it. Good day, Eve." Mother came to kiss her cheek, and Eve hugged Her. Betty retrieved the slipper.

Adam stumbled out just after Mother slipped it back on her foot.

"Ah. Until tomorrow, love." Mother kissed his cheek and wrinkled her nose. "You scratch," She complained. Adam rubbed his cheek on his mother's until She swatted him and turned to the door of the suite. "Take care," were Her final words.

He turned back to the closet, but Eve jumped up to grab his arm. "Come, eat," she bid him, pulling his hand all the way to the table and pushing him into a chair when he didn't sit right away. "You're still half asleep, aren't you? Should I let you go back to bed?"

He smiled to Betty, who poured him tea. "No, I'm up now and should be up anyway." Eve was still holding his hand, and he moved his fingers against hers. She blushed again. "So, what are we going to do today?" he asked.

"I was hoping you might know. It seems we have been left to our own devices." She ate with one hand, still holding his.

"Indeed? Oh right, the visit to Charleston. That would be today, wouldn't it?" He scratched his chin with his free hand.

Eve, curious, put her lips to his cheek. "They do scratch," she said with a chuckle.

He pulled her into his lap and rubbed his chin on her face, too, until she was giggling and fighting him off.

"Should I leave, Most High?" Betty asked with a smile.

"Not before you shave him," Eve complained, still struggling. Adam laughed, letting her go. "We could visit James and Delilah again this afternoon," Eve suggested.

"I was thinking we might visit the lab," Adam suggested as Betty applied the lather. Eve watched, still fascinated.

"Is that difficult?" she asked Betty.

"Not especially. You just have to angle it right. If you miss and get the angle too shallow, you can always lather and repeat, Most High."

She looked to Adam's eyes and bit her lip, wanting to try. He closed his eyes and whispered, "I must be infatuated. Yes, you can try. Please don't hurt me," he whimpered at the end.

Eve jumped to Betty's side. "You're sure you don't mind?" she asked Betty.

"Why should *she* mind?" Adam asked snidely. "It's my face!"

Eve chuckled. "Because it's her duty, her service." How was it he didn't understand? "She takes pride in it. Thank you," Eve said, taking the blade from her. Betty bent and stepped back just a pace, still grinning. "No, come closer," Eve urged. "Like this?" she put the blade at the angle she believed she had seen.

"Yes, but you want to start in other direction. It goes against the curl of the hair, making the shave closer to the skin."

"I see." Eve flipped the blade over and started high on Adam's cheek. She held his eyes for minute before looking back to the blade and scraping it very slowly over his skin. She noticed his eyes close. He was holding his breath. She started another strip without a break. He gasped, and she lifted the knife quickly to prevent a nick. "You need to hold still," she chided.

He put his hand to his cheek and pulled it back, looking for blood. She sighed and straightened his head to finish. He pulled his lips in as she took the hair under his nose. Leaning over him, her hair brushed his cheek. He closed his eyes again.

Eve wiped the blade and then the remaining lather from his face. She kissed his now smooth skin and murmured, "Much better."

He turned to her, putting his lips to hers. She sighed and leaned into his kiss, finding herself in his lap.

When she opened her eyes, Betty was gone. "So," she said not making any move to rise. It felt so nice to be in his arms.

"So," he echoed, brushing a hand through her hair.

"What are we going to do with ourselves this morning?" she asked.

*

She both wanted to please him and learn something new. There was no answer he could give that wouldn't have her leaping from the chair, eager to partake.

Adam shook his head a little. What had he done to have such a wonderful woman in his life? He kissed her once more, lightly. "How about the library? The lab is occupied. Unless you'd like to sit in on Ernst Peter's class? I must say, I'm curious to sit in on a discussion between the two of you."

She rose and headed to her room. "Perhaps this afternoon then? I find I monopolize the class, and that doesn't do for them."

"Really?" he asked, rising to follow.

"Yes," she said with a giggle. "The point of the class is to think for yourself, not have answers handed to you. My answers seem to stifle those of the others. They don't discuss as openly."

"You intimidate them," he said, putting his arms around her when she stopped at the wardrobe. "You intimidate me sometimes." He put his nose into her hair, nuzzling.

"Why do I think you don't want to go anywhere this morning?" she asked with a smile.

He let his thumbs stroke her belly while his lips found her neck. “Oh, I’m sure I’ll get to wanting to go somewhere. I’m just not done enjoying being here yet.”

She shivered in his arms, leaning her head to expose more of her throat. “Well, I can certainly take some time to fully experience this moment,” she teased in return.

He took one last deep breath, before straightening himself and taking one hand from her hip to pull out his clothes. She chose her gown once she saw what he was doing. His hand slid down and up her thigh as she stretched to reach down the gown.

He had taken out plain black. It would be an excellent choice if they did go to the lab this afternoon. He kissed her cheek before turning to go and she rubbed her cheek along his.

He pulled the shirt on and Betty held his jacket for him as he changed pants. He took the jacket, and was still adjusting the collar when Eve emerged.

Stepping out, she was pinning his favour to her dress. He came forward and put his hands to it. So near those breasts, round, perfect... He shook his head. Had he ever been so single minded before, so easily distracted? Was she put off by him? Did she want him to leave her be?

“You are sure?” he asked suddenly.

“Am I sure?” she asked, tipping her head to look into his still downcast eyes.

“About me. Are you sure you wouldn’t rather...”

She chuckled very quietly and took his hand. She put it to her chest, between her breasts, just below them. He tried to pull his eyes away, failing at first.

“I’m sure I wouldn’t be here without you,” she answered. His hand rested on the medallion of the Second, the lion-heart. She deserved it. She had earned it.

“But you are here now. You owe me nothing,” he said in honesty. She was not beholden to him in any way. She was entitled to everything that came with it, worthy of it.

*

Eve didn't answer immediately. She wanted to say she owed him everything, but seemed to know this was not the correct answer. She let rationale lead her. She had earned what she now held. She couldn't quite make herself accept that, but it was obvious all the other elite did. What was the correct response?

She opened her mouth twice. *I give you everything,* she was about to say once, but stopped herself again. *But I want more from you,* was also stopped before spoken.

"I don't want to be here without you," she finally whispered. "I wouldn't want to be here without you." She looked to his expression. Was this right? What he needed to hear?

"How was I here without you?" he answered and kissed her again.

Eve selected a logic dissertation from the shelves of the library and took the chair next to Adam. She made her way quickly through the first pages and then slowed to a crawl as she got into the meat of the argument.

"What are you reading?" He looked over her arm.

The Nature of Thought. It's a dissertation on the incorrect assessments commonly made by those beginning with false assumptions. Then, I hope, it will discuss the ways to minimize the likelihood of doing so. Right here, he is demonstrating some of the most common mistakes made by starting with faulty logic."

His brow crinkled, seeming puzzled, or as though he'd tasted something bitter. The more she watched him, the more she noticed. Why was Adam shifting so much? Was his chair uncomfortable? It was that bed. He really shouldn't be sleeping on it. Maybe he needed to stretch.

"What are you reading?" she finally asked.

"Nothing," he muttered.

"Really? Because it looks like a book to me."

"Was that my mother? That sounded like my mother." Adam looked over his shoulders as though he really expected the High One to step out from a corner.

Eve laughed. "Seriously, what are you reading?" She tipped the book to read the spine. "Oh! I remember that one. That's the one that taught me how to make salt."

"There is nothing about *salt* in this book," he complained. "I looked."

Was he pouting? She couldn't resist; she reached over and put a fingertip to the exposed lip, pulling it down slightly. He smiled and pulled her finger into his mouth. She gasped and pulled it back quickly, looking around. That was decidedly inappropriate for public. She swatted him. "No, nothing about *salt.* But if you look..." She flipped through to the page on mixing acid and base solutions. "You can find the clues."

Adam read the page skeptically. It spoke about putting lime into vinegar, as Eve had suggested, but that these crystals were weak and fragile. The author posited that the strength of the acid may have been the problem.

"And you remembered this?" he wondered.

"No. I remembered this when I was in Ernst Peter's logic class. That was when I realized that the weak crystals bore the same properties as salt. Following the posit, a stronger acid should yield stronger crystals, even more closely resembling salt."

"You are amazing. You know that don't you?" She blushed and looked away from his scrutiny. "I'm serious. How do you do all of this in your head? You've never really used a lab, have you? Have you ever experimented?"

She shook her head. "No. I was examined by the Ernst, but that was using existing protocols. I built a grinder, but that was as far as you could say I 'experimented.'"

"You built a grinder?"

"I was asked to assemble a steam engine. Then I was asked to use it. So I built a mechanism that would move the pestle on the mortar. It didn't really grind, but it worked somewhat." She wrinkled her nose a little in distaste. Surely she could have done something more elegant.

Adam nodded, still awestruck. "Well, I don't need this anymore. Can you read to me from that? Maybe hearing it will make more sense."

"Oh, well, all right." She looked around to make sure she wouldn't be disturbing anyone, but only one other elite was in the room, on the far side. The Librarians wouldn't be distracted by her reading.

She read slowly, digesting her own words as she read. She found she was able to grasp much more quickly this way. She hoped her parsing and emphasis made it easier for Adam to follow the thoughts as well. Could he see the groupings, the categories, the characteristics?

The noon bell startled them both when it rang. "I suppose we should have our lunch?" Eve rose from her chair.

*

Adam stretched as he followed. How long had they been sitting here? How many pages had she read? He looked to her hand as saw they were over halfway through the book.

"Yes, lunch." He took her hand and led her to their suite.

They decided to stop briefly at the lab along their way. Eve was introduced to Ernst Derek at last.

"A pleasure, Most High. I understand you have some theories to test with us?"

She looked to Adam, seeming puzzled. "I'm not sure I'll be doing so today, Honoured. I think I'll observe again, for now."

He frowned very slightly, disappointed. She had so many wonderful ideas in her books, so much that could be proven. Another day, perhaps.

"Of course," Derek answered. He led her among the benches where various elite were testing their own theories. Most were

Princes or Ducat, of an age with himself, older than Eve, younger than Derek. They all seemed eager.

She watched one Ducat trying to melt his minerals together. Acrid smoke started to fill the air. Eve quickly began wafting the smoke to the window, taking the beaker with her. The Ducat opened his mouth but made no move to stop her. She left the beaker on the sill and returned to his bench.

"What were you trying to accomplish?" she asked, looking over his ingredients. "Why were you melting sulphur?"

"I was trying to make an alloy," he explained.

Eve shook her head. "Sulphur is not a metal. If you want to try to add it to the matrix of a metal," she stopped, letting her thoughts run. Adam watched the green of her eyes shift shades, first light green like new leaves, then the dark of evergreens. "I don't think it will have the result that you desire," she warned, but proceeded to place a crucible with nickel shavings from his bench directly into the fire.

Then she used the mortar and pestle to grind the sulphur as finely as she could. She carried the mortar to the fire and watched for the melting to occur. As soon as the metal was liquid she poured the sulphur in and used the tongs to swirl the concoction. Then she held the crucible in the water barrel to cool. She turned the result out on the bench with a hard jolt. The block of yellow threaded nickel skittered across the surface.

The Ducat reached for it, and she snagged his hand. "Fool! It's still hot."

"It didn't react," he complained.

She sighed. "Of course it didn't. Was that what you desired? Both these substances are inert, why would melting them cause them to react?" she asked. He had no answer of course.

Ernst Derek whispered to Adam, distracting his observation, "I wish she'd stopped some of the fools in her class."

"You need both materials to be in a state of change if you want them to interact," Eve declared.

She looked at the two she had, then to the window where she'd left the smoking beaker. Recovering it, she placed a lid with a tube on it, feeding the smoke into a second container of water, bubbling gas. What was she doing?

"Put the shavings in there," she ordered, nodding to the beaker of water. The Ducat complied and the bubbles began to attack the nickel. It wasn't obvious, but seemed likely, that they would eat away the metal. She stopped and clapped her hands. "I don't know what the result will be, but this should prove much more successful.

She pulled the flask from the brazier before it could overheat. She left the bench with a quick clap on the shoulder for her lab partner. Then she walked back to Adam and Derek.

"That was interesting." Her eyes had lightened again; Adam believed she was seeking a new idea.

"Indeed. How do we make alloys if metals are non-reactive," Adam asked her now.

"Oh, when they are both metals, the result is entirely different. They are able to blend matrices in many cases. Sulphur is *not* a metal; therefore the same rules cannot apply." She looked to another desk where crystals were being formed, very slowly. "May I?" she asked the Ducati at the bench.

"Please," she said stepping aside.

Eve placed the beaker over the brazier swirling very gently. She grabbed a glass rod from the bench and scratched the edge of beaker as she continued to swirl, then she spun the rod in the solution once before returning to scratching.

"What are you doing?" the Ducati asked.

Distilling, Adam thought.

"Removing excess water to saturate the solution, and trying..." her voice strained a little as she scratched the edge of the beaker again, "to create a surface for formation to initiate. Ah!" she said happily, setting the beaker back on the bench. The crystals were spreading much more quickly across the beaker.

"Thank you," the Ducati said with a small bow.

"What are they?" Eve asked, looking at the desk. The crystals were purple. "You must let me read your notes when you have described this." She pointed back to the beaker.

"Of course, Most High," she said with another bow.

"Let's get you out of here before you scare off all Derek's students." Adam smiled at her.

Eve blushed and cast her eyes down. She wasn't used to people being intimidated by her. It had always been the other way around.

She nodded to Derek before departing. "Why did you tell him I have theories to test? I don't."

"You don't intend to make your salt?" he was astounded.

"No. I know how to do it, why would I before there was need?" she asked now.

"To be sure the theory is sound." He regretted it as soon as he said it.

"The theory is sound. That solution will make crystals. Whether or not they are a good substitute for natural salt is uncertain, but it would make salt-like crystals. Why waste the supplies if the salt is not necessary?" She shook her head.

A waste of supplies? If she could document a new salt source, that would not be a waste. Adam could not follow her reasoning now. It was usually so clear, so easy to follow.

*

They halted in front of the carved door. "You're sure you want to do this?" Adam asked.

"Of course. Don't you?" Eve asked, hand on his arm.

"Sure." He steeled himself and knocked.

"Come in," Maria called.

Adam held the door for Eve, who was assaulted as soon as she was spotted.

"Eve!"

"Eve! Adam!" Delilah ran to her brother as James had already clasped onto Eve.

"Well, hello," Eve said rumpling James' hair. His head was only a little lower than her own. "Did we interrupt anything?" Eve asked Maria when it became obvious James wasn't letting go.

He did at her words. "We were playing." Eve followed him to a board. It held twelve men of two colors. This would be one of the lesser games. "Delilah was nearly beaten. I'm going to win!" James declared happily.

Delilah took a seat on one side of the board with a grunt and moved a piece, capturing one of James'. His mouth opened a little in surprise before he moved again.

Adam leaned into Eve's ear. "The attacks are the same, but they have no defence. The object is to capture the opponent's Bishop, rather than to acquire the goal."

She nodded in comprehension. He watched her eyes darken as she followed the game. Abruptly she rose from beside him and whispered in Delilah's ear, "You can take his Bishop in five attacks. Find them."

Adam looked back to the board. He saw the sequence now. Eve returned and took a seat in his lap. She was coming to enjoy that seat. "May I have the pleasure of the next game?" she asked.

"Will you embarrass me in front of my siblings? The ones who still think I'm smart?" he asked sulkily.

She laughed and hugged his neck. He closed his eyes. "I will not simply hand you the win," she assured him, backing up again. "But you are more familiar with this game than I am. The advantage is yours."

Adam looked to his siblings. Both were intent on the board, so he kissed Eve, holding her tightly. "The only advantage I have is possibly the ability to scramble your wits." He kissed her again and traced a hand down her spine making Eve tremble and sigh. When she opened her eyes they were blue.

Adam heard giggling and quickly moved his hands back to the arms of the chair.

"He really does like her," Delilah whispered to James.

"It's still weird. She's our sister now."

"But she isn't," Delilah reminded him. "Not really. Not the way Adam is."

Eve searched Adam's eyes while listening to the commentary. As though she wondered if he thought of her as a sister. He certainly cared for her as much as Delilah, but more, in a different way. He wanted her, always. He wouldn't let her go if he could help it. She blushed and looked away.

Delilah clapped her hands, "I win!" She jumped up and twirled around. "I win! I never win! Thank you, Eve!" She hugged Eve from behind.

"You cheated!" James accused, looking from Delilah to Eve.

"I only told her she could win in five moves. I didn't tell her which five. May I play?" she asked now.

Delilah clapped her hands again. Adam nudged James out of his place. "Unless you want to challenge her?" Adam asked. James quickly rose.

"Supper, both of you," Maria reminded them, pointing to the table where their meal was laid out.

Once the board was reset, Eve quickly chose a piece and moved it. Adam blanched slightly at how avidly she entered the game, how green her eyes had become. He brushed her fingers after he had moved his piece, trying to distract again. He hoped he wouldn't embarrass himself.

The game was not short and lasted until James and Delilah returned from eating. They questioned Eve about her duties as a Server, her own parents, science and the lab. James had reached Ernst Derek's class and was most interested in this now. Her family and friends from her previous life still stung very slightly to remember, but Eve was happy to have the opportunity. She'd rarely thought of them outside dinner, when she saw her friends among the Servers.

The post noon bell had just rung when Eve's eyes lit up. "I take it I've lost," Adam said. Indeed he now saw that she would take his Bishop in three attacks. He knocked the piece over. "Just as well. We need to prepare for dinner."

"Must I sit at the High Table alone?" she asked as they returned to their suite. "I don't know if I can do it. Isn't there some way?" she pleaded, nervous.

"Once dinner begins you may invite me to sit with you," Adam offered.

She let out a sigh of relief. "Thank you."

"The pleasure will be all mine," Adam assured her.

*

Adam accompanied Eve to her room and chose her gown and robe, black with scarlet. She was still intimidated by the elegance of her clothing but changed quickly once Adam had exited. She took a seat with Betty while he changed.

"Thank you, again, for this morning," Eve told Betty.

Betty smiled and dipped quickly, never really interrupting her hands in Eve's hair. "I think you enjoy that duty even more than I, Most High. Shall I leave it to you in future?"

Eve giggled. "You and Mother are horrid gossips, I think. So what are your wagers?" she asked.

"Wagers, High One?"

"Come, you must have a wager on how long until one of us crosses this imaginary line that divides us. I'm sure Mother has a date in her mind."

Betty laughed loudly, but she sobered quickly when Adam emerged. "Indeed," she said calmly. "She believes you will wait until after her return."

"For what?" Adam asked, eyeing the women.

Eve turned to look at Betty. "You think before?" she said incredulously. She twisted forward again with a sulky expression.

Adam's eyes were fixed on her lower lip. Eve noticed the glitter in Betty's eyes as she painted Eve's face. Eve flicked her eyes, careful not to twitch, and Adam continued to gaze at her. Eve sighed very quietly. Perhaps Betty's wager was the wiser.

Eve had to carefully remind herself not to hold Adam's hand through dinner. It wasn't acceptable in the hall. Instead she touched her foot to his leg once or twice when her nerves got the better of her; a reminder that she wasn't alone and a thank you to him.

There was much whispering when Eve invited Adam to sit at her table. She could make out parts, but not the whole. She gathered that most thought she was making a poor choice.

"You'll have men approaching you in the days to come. Mothers will press their sons to try to take my place now that you've made it clear," Adam explained to her. "I should have made that evident when you asked."

Eve wasn't worried. There was only one man she wanted. The others would be disappointed.

After dinner, she took the silk rag from her pocket to tend the board. Her duty done, she walked alone back to the suite. Adam had elected not to wait for her, instead preparing for bed while her room was unoccupied.

Unfortunately, someone else had decided to wait for her in his stead. "He isn't worthy of you," a male voice called from the atrium as she left the hall.

"Who is there?" she asked, turning around. "Who is here?"

Prince Louis stepped from the shadows to approach her. "I have more honour than he does now, and I came for you first," he claimed, reaching for her wrist.

"You came for me first, but I was never yours," she replied, snapping her hand back. She turned to head down the hall. His hand came to her arm again, and she yanked it back. "Let go of me," she demanded, pressing her elbow to his ribs.

"I was merely attempting to help you to your rooms," he lied, pressing his hand to her waist to guide her feet. His nose was at her neck. She threw her head back and heard him cry as she connected with his face.

"Keep your hands off me," she demanded, whirling to face him again. "You have no claim to me. You never did. You will treat me as my station demands."

"Your station," he said snidely, wiping the trickle of blood from his lip where it was split. "You are still a Server, girl. Run to your fallen Second. I will come for you again."

Louis turned and walked away from her. The insult to her was severe. She should report it, but she just wanted desperately to forget the entire encounter. She strode quickly for her suite.

Eve shook slightly as she closed the door to the suite behind her. The closet door was closed, and she made her way to her room. Adam wasn't there either, apparently already in bed. Eve changed quickly and knocked on his door in her nightdress.

"Adam? Can I talk with you?"

He heard the tremble in her voice and quickly opened the door. "Eve. What happened?" he asked, wrapping his arms around her.

Relief swamped her as his warmth surrounded her. It made her feel safe and wonderful and terrible all at the same time. She sat on the edge of his cot and wept for a while in fury and embarrassment.

"Prince Louis. He... he was waiting for me."

"Louis," he spat. Adam felt his blood boil. He was still trying to get to Eve. "That boy always did reach above his station. Don't worry Eve. Just tell Vanto Ethan-"

"No," she shook her head. "No. I don't think I can." She wrapped her arms around herself. "Stay with me? Talk with me? Help me forget?" she asked, looking up to him with sky blue eyes.

"Of course," he answered. He put one arm around her shoulders and guided her to her bed. "What do you want talk about?" he asked as he lifted her covers for her. He lay atop them on the opposite side, rolling onto his shoulder to see her.

She did the same, propping her chin on an elbow. "Tell me what it was like when you were little?" Her voice was still very heavy.

"Well, it was happy. I lived with Uncle Albert and Aunt Maria and Martina. She was still a baby. Uncle Albert would often take us with him when he travelled."

Eve watched as Adam rolled to his back and reminisced on the sights he had seen, the places he had visited. He, too, described buildings that were taller than trees, but looked like skeletons with all their walls and windows gone. He described black, tar-like ground that went in straight lines for miles and miles, but often led to nothing. Eve closed her eyes, trying to imagine the wonders for herself. It wasn't long before she did see herself among them, but only in her dream.

*

She woke and was happy to see Adam hadn't left. He was still asleep on the other side of her bed. She shuffled over slightly to touch his brow, smoothing the lines from his frown, then shifted a little further onto his outstretched arm. She put her fingers into the hair curling on his chest. Her father was the only other man she'd seen shirtless, and he did not have hair on his chest. It was soft and thick and dark brown. She noticed the line of hair trailed down his belly and quickly brought her hands and eyes back up, blushing furiously.

Which, of course, was the moment he woke enough to pull his arms in, pressing her to his chest.

"Good morning?" she squeaked.

"Mmm?" he mumbled, pressing one hand to his eyes. He froze and released his hold on her. Chuckling, he asked. "Did I startle you? You seem to have been the one awake," he teased now.

She blushed again and nestled into him. "I was."

He sighed. "I think I could like waking up like this." He put his cheek to her hair. She fit so perfectly into the curve of his arm; her ear just above his heart.

She giggled feeling his bristles on her scalp. "You need a shave again."

"Every morning," he muttered, stretching now.

Eve bit her lip as she watched. She couldn't resist putting a hand to his chest again as it expanded with his movement.

"Well," she said as she pulled her hand back. "I hope this means you might take me up on my offer for the bed. I didn't even know you were still here until I opened my eyes. The mattress is so large."

He narrowed his eyes slightly. "It seems you did prove your point. I will consider it. I must admit, I'm a little afraid of what my mother will say to me when she finds out." He groaned. "She will as soon as she gets back. Betty's out there now with breakfast. I bet the closet door is open too." He covered his eyes with his hand.

Eve pressed her cheek on his chest. The hair tickled her nose. It was nice. "I don't care what they say." She closed her eyes and listened to his heartbeat, his breathing.

*

"You are a brave woman," Adam wrapped an arm around her. They were going to be unbearable in their taunts. Mother's would be vocal, but worse would be the silent glint in Betty's eye. He never understood how that look from her always said so much more than his mother, but it did. "I suppose we should get this over with. She's going to know regardless."

He sat up, and Eve followed him out the door. Their breakfast was on the table along with the shaving supplies, but no Betty.

Eve flushed and looked at her toes. "Well, I guess that solves that problem."

"Where is she?" he asked, looking around corners. He even peeped into his mother's room.

"She's giving us time alone," Eve said, sitting down to her breakfast and pouring tea. "It is very kind of her; forgoing her duty for us." She poured for Adam, too, as he came to sit.

"Kind of her? She has a free morning. It seems to benefit her as well."

Eve shook her head. "It is an honour to serve. We take pride in every task assigned to us. Well, if we are worthy of our duty we do. We do not seek opportunities to shirk those duties. We try to find ways to improve our service. It was likely difficult for her to take herself from the suite before seeing to you and me. I will thank her at lunch." Eve sipped her tea.

Adam wolfed down his eggs and sipped his tea. Servants really thought like that? Well, not all of them; she admitted as much. But most of them? He remembered that she saw her new position as a duty, a service. She intended to take pride in every aspect of her new place. He smiled at her and took her hand. She smiled back.

"She noticed I enjoy shaving you and offered to give me this duty. If you agree, that is." Eve cocked an eyebrow, hoping he would.

"You did an excellent job yesterday. I won't argue," he said, pulling her to her feet as she grabbed the cream.

"How do you eat so fast?" she asked as she moved to his side.

There was a brush in the jar to apply the cream, but she took it out and dipped her fingers in. She started under his chin and brought her fingers up and over it, leaving a smooth smear of cream behind them. His eyes closed as she did, indulging in the slick, soft feeling of her fingers. She kissed his lips, then dipped her fingers again and ran her hand over the left side of his throat up to his jaw. She was leaning over him, her breath on his face. It was completely unlike when Betty brushed it on. His entire face felt on fire, and he wondered if he were blushing. He clenched his jaw, fighting the desire growing in him.

"Cold?" she asked, dipping again.

"No," his answered, voice raspy.

"Good," she said and repeated her application on the right. She made a circle over his right cheek, spreading the cream evenly over the entire surface although his whiskers were fewer there. Her touch, he would never have enough of it. On his face, his chest... His mouth opened, breathing in her scent, as she leaned over again to apply to the left. His hands found her hips and pulled her into his lap. Kissing her, he spread cream all over her face as well.

She laughed. "I don't need to shave, thank you."

He opened his eyes to her face, her beautiful blue eyes. Light blue, not deep. He still didn't know the significance, but it seemed the darker blue followed her stronger emotions. He shook his head banishing the fire from his chest, his groin. He was only partially successful, enough to try to go on. "I'm sorry, Eve. Please, continue." He leaned back, knuckles gripping his knees.

She smoothed the disturbed cream and applied a small dab under his nose. Then she kissed the tip of it before picking up the blade and towel. "Ready?" she asked.

He closed his eyes. "Yes." He wasn't, not at all. He had no idea how he would bear having her so close and keeping his hands to himself.

"Are you sure this is all right, Adam?" she asked.

"Please, continue," he said through clenched teeth.

Eve obeyed and leaned over to put the blade to his left cheek. Adam sighed heavily, hands twitching to reach for her. In three quick strokes, the cheek was finished. He took another breath in relief, as she wiped the blade and straightened. She gave the same to the right cheek, reaching over him again.

Her breath was in his ear now. He was losing his mind. She had no idea what she was doing to him, did she? She didn't know how much he wanted to take her back to her room right now. He balled his fists tighter and clenched his jaw again. He could not afford to step wrongly now. She trusted him.

She put a finger to his lips before bringing the blade under his nose. He pulled his lips in, and she pulled the blade very gently along. She tipped his chin up to expose his throat and he swallowed.

"Don't be afraid. I won't hurt you," she whispered.

"I trust you, Eve. It's me I don't trust," he mumbled in reply.

She stopped in the process of putting the blade to his throat. He wondered why, but he only had time to open his eyes before she pressed the blade to the near side. The angle was different under his chin, and she carefully turned the blade at the curve of his jaw and continued to his ear. She ran her finger over her work to check.

Adam grabbed her hand. "I think I need a break," he said breathless. "Excuse me."

Eve stood, perplexed. Adam entered the closet and closed the door, shutting himself in the dark. He flopped stomach down on the bed and tried to regulate his breathing. He now had cream all over his arm, too. He didn't care much about that at all. It meant she was going to have to reapply it. He groaned, thinking about that and rolling to his back.

"Adam?" she asked through the door. "Are you all right? Is there anything I can do?"

He thought briefly through some of the things she could do and then groaned again. "No, no. I'll be fine. Just, another minute, please." He sat up now with his head in his hands. He took a few deep breaths, feeling his pulse slow. A bit of water on his face would help. He rose and opened the door. She was there with a worried expression on her face.

"I'm fine, really, Eve. I'm just going to splash my face." She followed him into her room and continued to observe him as he poured water into the bowl. He put cold wet hands to his face, and it did help.

"Did I do something wrong, Adam?" she asked. "You don't need a break when Betty does this."

I'm not in love with Betty, he thought. He took a deep breath.

"It's just... It's you Eve." He took her face in his hands and kissed her, his lips pulling hers apart. She gasped and put her hands to his shoulders kissing him back, putting her tongue to his bottom lip. He groaned. Maybe she did understand. "You're sure?" he asked again.

She nodded, eyes wide, and he kissed her again. Her lips, her jaw, her throat, her collarbone. He covered her exposed skin with kisses for several minutes before letting her go.

"I think I've quelled the monster for a little while," he admitted.

"I'm going to like shaving you," she declared, pulling him behind her back to the chair.

Eve managed to finish Adam's shave. The monster needed quelling again after though. Eve's heart pounded loudly, threatening to break through her chest when Adam's hands roamed over her torso. Adam was sure he wouldn't stop short of tearing the filmy cloth from her. They were both wrong.

When Eve backed away, desperate for air, Adam again saw the woman he admired within the woman he desired. He shifted his attention, with some success, to crave her mind again. He asked her to read from her notes, to discuss them with him.

If the elite are willing to exchange self for honour, is honour separate from self? Do servants have a sense of self if it is not tied to their service? Is their self separate from their duty? What portion is held within each?

"Do you think I'd be someone else if I was Adam, the Server, rather than Vanto Adam?" he asked her.

"I know you would be. Just as I am not the same Eve I was a few weeks ago. I am more and less than I was. I was a Server. A portion of my identity, not an insignificant portion, came from that reference. It dictated how I regarded the world around me, what I did, even how I thought."

"How you thought?" he asked. "You believe you don't think the same? Today's Eve couldn't reason out how to make salt or that giant buildings must be rooted?"

"Of course I could, but I wouldn't."

He clutched his head. "What?"

"Those reasonings were the direct result of my education and reading. The Second doesn't attend class, doesn't spend time looking at new studies in the library. She, or he, doesn't have a mother in the kitchen for whom she designs pots. She doesn't look at the honours traded over the Cargon table and see a fate worse than her own. I am not who I was."

"But even if you hadn't become Second, you wouldn't be who you were. Our perspectives are constantly changing by what we learn."

She shook her head. "You are right that I would not be who I was, but my perspective was not changed by what I learned; only clarified by it. I was a better servant, able to provide more, improve the service of others. That is where I was. Some of the same ends are being met, but as *you* informed me, I no longer serve. My perspective was changed when my tree changed."

"Tree?" Adam asked confused.

Eve flipped to her private lessons from Peter and read, "One bloom opens on a tree. Is the tree female, male or both? One bloom will not tell, many are needed. An individual does not describe the world she exists in, the others around her do.

"I am the bloom on the tree. When I was on the servants' tree, I was a Server and that was my world. Now I am Second and the elite are my world."

"Or both! You wrote here: *or both*. Isn't it one world? Didn't we exist together before?"

Eve looked at him blandly. Adam was brighter than this. He knew the answer.

"No. I can't agree with that. You were in my world before."

"Had you ever noticed me before I moved a piece on the Cargon table?"

Adam's brow furrowed. It couldn't be. How could two worlds overlap so completely and never touch? How could she be nothing there and everything here? It made no sense.

He stared into her bright green eyes searching for an answer, a denial.

"I didn't see you either," she admitted quietly. "I knew there was a Second. I knew his name was Adam and that he had dark hair. However, I knew the Princes and Ducat at my tables better than you, and I only knew them as white, red or both. I knew you kept our world running and that my small service helped you do so. I didn't need more. I wanted more, certainly, but I wanted greater service, not an escape from it. I never dreamed of such a thing. I was thinking I might be a teacher of servants, or a Librarian, especially once I was granted access."

"You were to be," Adam whispered, horrified. "That was Mother's intention. She has groomed the most recent Librarians."

Eve smiled. "I think I would have made a good Librarian."

"But you can be so much more," Adam argued, seizing the tops of her arms.

She giggled. "Now I can. I can be Second. I can serve so much more here, and I will be a credit to my duty." She closed her eyes and beamed. "I will bring all that I am and all that I have to the High One. I will be Her right hand. I will fulfill whatever purpose She has for me, and, I pray, if the worst should befall..." She shook her head, tears in her eyes. "I can't even imagine myself in Her place. That is why I was shocked and terrified when She left. I can serve Her. Without Her, who would I serve? All?"

Adam couldn't speak. She was a Server. She thought herself elite now that that was the world she inhabited, but it would never be true. She would be a servant to all, if it came to that.

"I think that is no small part of the reason I cannot let you go. You would be my Second, and then you would be High One," she continued after a pause.

"No," he whispered and took her hands. "No, you would serve all, just as you said." His voice broke, but he forced the rest out. "You would be the best of High Ones because of it."

"Adam? Have I upset you?" she asked, putting a hand to his cheek. "That day will not come," she said cheerfully, kissing him. "Bianca, Mother, She isn't going anywhere. Our children will be acceptable Seconds before anything befalls Her." She laughed.

Our children, he thought. She was certain. She had been from the beginning. Why did he question her? Why did he believe she would change her mind? Even if she changed her perspective enough to marry another, and he doubted she ever would, she would never let go of him. Bringing her into his world, he had given her his life, his purpose. It shouldn't surprise him that his heart went with it. They were one now, more completely than any ceremony or title could ever grant.

"Adam? Did I upset you?" she asked again. "I didn't mean to imply that you mightn't have other ..."

He kissed her to stop her words. How could she think such a thing? He couldn't imagine it any longer. From the moment his eyes had met hers, he knew only one woman had any hold on him, one woman he would be attracted to, one woman he would ever love.

Eve smiled against his lips. She had disturbed him, but his response soothed her. He was not offended.

"Never. Never suggest that I would be with anyone aside from you." He kissed her again, deeply now.

She hadn't expected that. It seemed obvious, as the situation was clarified, that the elite did not often form tight bonds, not when honour could so easily strain them. Adam, himself, had told her that it was difficult. She had never expected him to tie himself to her. She had hoped for it, of course; hoped for a love as strong as that between her parents. She felt as he did. She would never be with another, but for him to feel the same was almost impossible.

The longer he kissed her, the closer they came to those future children. “Adam,” she whispered as he knelt and kissed her abdomen and thighs. “Adam,” she repeated, a little louder. His hands traced her ribcage and came to rest on her breasts. “Adam!” she cried, clasping his hair and pulling his head back gently to look at her. “Not today,” she said with a low chuckle. “We have years. I was only kissed for the first time a few months ago. I’m going to need a little more time.”

He blushed scarlet and moved to sit in a chair on the far side of the room.

“Oh no you don’t,” she said. “You don’t feel badly,” she commanded, rising and moving to his side. She tipped his chin up just as she had to shave him and kissed his lips gently. “I asked you to stop so you wouldn’t feel badly. If you want to go back and take your time getting to that point,” she suggested, kissing him again.

“You are a different person, aren’t you?” he asked.

She smiled. “I am some of the same. After all, I am not completely defined by my world, and neither are you.”

He took her hand from his chin and kissed her palm. “I love you, Eve.”

“And I love you, Adam.”

They were still in their bedclothes when Betty arrived with lunch. She didn’t speak as she presented their meal.

Eve broke the silence. “Thank you so much for this morning, Betty. I appreciate it more than you know.”

She bowed deeply. “I think I have an idea how much you appreciated it, Most High,” she said quietly enough that Adam didn’t make out all the words. Eve giggled.

That afternoon Eve joined Adam in discussions with Ernst Peter. He quizzed them both endlessly. Adam was quiet for most of their exchanges, unless Eve pulled him in, asking his opinion.

Adam was most struck when Eve began questioning Peter. "If the road continues into the distance with no end, how can one know one will ever reach it?"

"All roads must end. Some have ends that are less discernible than others, but all roads DO end."

Eve nodded at this. "Even if it ends only to continue again?"

"Seemingly without stopping, yes...."

"And are all roads navigable in both directions?" she asked next.

"Hmmm." Ernst Peter closed his eyes. "No. Some roads are destroyed behind one."

Eve nodded again. "Indeed, making return impossible. No," she corrected herself, "not impossible, but a different route must be taken."

"Yes," Peter agreed. "Sometimes home cannot be reached simply by turning around. New roads, new ways, must be found."

"And sometimes one can find themselves home again without really knowing how they reached it."

Adam was sure they weren't talking about roads anymore, but he wasn't entirely sure what they were talking about. Life? Duty? Roles? It was hard to say.

*

They returned to the suite to find Mother having her hair washed. "I hear you two enjoyed your free time," She said with a broad smile.

Eve blushed and smiled broadly. "I hope Betty wagered something valuable." She stepped forward to kiss Mother's cheek as she laughed. "Adam? Help me choose something to wear to dinner?" she asked over her shoulder, heading to her room.

She heard Mother suggest, "Or something to take off?" and chuckled. Betty's cackle joined Mother's when Adam entered Eve's room.

She had already pulled off her robe and was pulling out various dresses in an effort to choose one. "Don't be embarrassed," she ordered him. “They’re happy for us, and happy people laugh.” She held a deep green dress up but put it aside.

Adam pulled out a white dress and purple robe. Eve’s eyes went wide. “You’re sure?” she asked. Purple was an uncommon colour.

“I’m sure. You will look spectacular.” He selected his own clothes and moved to leave.

“No, wait,” she stopped him, stepping behind the open door of the wardrobe. “There, now we can both change.” She stepped around, finding him in blue and cream. “Do you mind?” she asked, holding out her pin to him with a smile.

“You trust me too much,” he said, pinning it to her dress. She grabbed his hands when he finished and held them to her, not ready to let him go. He kissed her lightly. “Betty will be waiting for you,” he said.

“Yes, yes. Dinner won’t wait,” she complained.

Eve was surprised to find someone waiting in the hall for her.

“Most High? May I offer you this token and accompany you?” The Ducat held a pink rose out to her. He was only a little older than Eve, probably about the same age as Adam, perhaps a little younger. He had dark hair and red-brown skin. His eyes were warm and danced with excitement.

Eve took the rose with a smile. “Thank you, Highness.” She held out her hand, and he took it on his arm.

“I apologize, Highness. I don’t know your name.” Eve was congenial.

“Evan, Most High. And it is a pleasure to make your acquaintance.” He lifted her hand to his lips, and Eve blushed. Evan walked her to the High Table and left her at her seat. “I hope to have the chance to see you again soon.”

Adam escorted Bianca to her seat and then turned to his own. Eve grabbed his hand and squeezed it quickly.

Others came throughout dinner. “Prince Darren, Most High,” he said as he handed her a pink peony.

"Ducat Glen," another introduced himself, giving her a pink tulip.

"Prince Ryan, Most High." He kissed her hand while producing a pink carnation. She made a small bouquet of the flowers and set them aside as the first course arrived.

"What happened last night?" Mother asked. "They seem to be almost stepping over each other to reach you."

"I couldn't bear to sit here alone, so I invited Adam to join me."

"Ah, yes. That would do it," Mother nodded. "You will have many more coming, I believe. They will all want you to consider their offers before you finally decide."

"Decide?"

"To marry Adam, of course. Inviting him to sit with you showed your interest in him. You must understand, Eve, that we are often placed in arranged marriages which benefit our families. You are not attached to anyone and in a place of high status. There is almost no one in this hall who wouldn't want to take their chance to attach themselves to you."

When the soup was cleared away more blooms were produced. A few more Princes and Ducat came forward, but soon it was the Most High stepping up. Eve blushed as more and more came, but made sure to smile to all.

"What am I supposed to do?" she asked Mother.

"What do you want to do?"

Eve had no idea. She wanted to give each of them the attention they deserved, but she certainly couldn't do that, there were so many! She was approached by a pair at the same time, Vanto Phillip and Vanto Stuart she recognized. She mused aloud, "I enjoy Cargon."

The men looked to one another and then Eve. She held out her hand expecting one or the other to take it. They turned and headed to the Cargon table.

Eve gasped. “That’s not what I meant,” she whispered to Mother.

“No, but this should be interesting.” At the end of the meal, Eve and the High One moved to watch the unfolding match. Surely her attentions were not enough to wager on. She held the blooms in her hand. Adam nodded to her before heading back to the suite. She would see him after the match was completed.

The game was interesting to watch; both were clearly worthy players. In the end, Vanto Phillip won. He took her hand and kissed it briefly, giving her both blooms. “Would you be willing to join me for lunch in the garden tomorrow?” he asked.

Eve’s eyes went wide. The garden? “I would. Thank you, Vanto.”

“Phillip,” he corrected.

“Phillip,” she agreed.

She waited with Mother while she tended the board. “This board will see much play over the next few weeks, I think.”

“Why?” Eve asked.

“Well, another will challenge Phillip tomorrow, and the night after, and the night after that. They took you at your words. You enjoy Cargon, so they will play for you.”

Eve hung her head. “What have I done?”

“A very good thing. I’ve never seen so many suitors for one hand. It was going to be very messy. This will help so much. They all respect the Game. Those unwilling to risk playing will simply forfeit their suit. This should work very well.”

Eve was thrilled to find Adam already in her bed when she returned to her room. “I hope I’m still welcome here,” he said shyly.

She leaned over to kiss him. “Always.” She changed behind the wardrobe door again and slipped in on the far side of the bed.

She woke with his breath in her ear. He was curled around her back, and his arm was wrapped around her chest. She sighed closing her eyes again. He was going to make it easier to remember where she woke in the mornings.

"Mmmm?" His hand squeezed her, and she giggled. "Oh, I'm sorry, Eve."

She grabbed his hand before he could pull it away. "Don't apologize," she chided. Then she rolled into his arms to kiss him again. "Sleep well?" she asked.

"Amazingly well," he answered.

"I'm glad." She stretched as she climbed out of bed.

Mother was at the table already and smiled broadly as they exited together. Eve sipped her tea and asked which meetings she would be attending today. She also mentioned that she would be lunching with Phillip. She noticed Adam's glower.

Eve used the brush to apply the lather today, hoping to take Adam's edge from him. Bianca took Betty to her room while Eve worked.

Adam sighed as soon as his mother left the table. "I thought she was going to watch us all morning."

Eve giggled while wiping off the blade. "Indeed, she likes to see you happy."

"She likes to see me uncomfortable," he muttered.

Eve laughed again. "Where are you lunching?" Adam asked.

"In the garden," she said shakily. She still wasn't sure it was a good idea. She finished his shave as she spoke. "I'm not sure how I will react, but, perhaps, it will be better this way. I have no association with my friends and Phillip. Unlike you," she smiled. "They know how I feel about you. I'd probably be terribly embarrassed, as well as uncomfortable, if I was lunching with you in the garden."

Adam took reassurance from that.

Her lunch meeting with Phillip was enjoyable. He was an excellent conversationalist. He spurred her into talking about some of her ideas regarding the tall buildings. As a historian, he was very interested in her theories. She found his tales of their construction both unbelievable and fantastic. Still, she had no better ideas of her own. She didn't linger, though, having meetings that afternoon.

That night, a Ducat challenged Phillip to a match. "I'm not sure this was a good thing," Eve moaned to Mother.

"It was. You'll see."

Phillip won the match and took her hand again. "May I walk you to your rooms?" he asked.

"Certainly," she agreed, walking with him through the corridor.

"I do hope you consider my offer," he murmured as he kissed her hand again at the door.

"I will think on it," she promised. She examined his lined face; he was much older than she. He was kind, though; she could tell by the deepest lines at his lips, laugh lines. She wondered what would make him laugh. She closed the door behind her.

Adam opened it while she was still leaning on it, and she fell into him. "I'm sorry!" she cried as he straightened her, laughing.

"Are you all right, Eve?" he saw the creases on her face.

"Can you explain to me why elite marry for honour? I like Phillip, but I don't love him. Why would I marry him?"

Adam sighed, "The elite want for very little. So we have built a system for ranking ourselves against one another."

He didn't add to his explanation, and Eve thought on that while changing into a nightdress. "But isn't this," she took his hand to show what she meant, "something to desire?"

He pulled her to him and tucked her under his chin. "It certainly is."

Eve was still confused, but also very comfortable and more than a little tired. She fell asleep thinking on adding up honours.

CHAPTER SEVEN

Eve and Adam lingered too long in bed the next morning. She hurried to change and ate quickly so she wouldn't miss her meeting with Mother. Adam took his time, knowing neither woman needed his advice any longer. What was he going to do to fill his days now? What was his purpose to be? He pulled Eve's notes to him after he was dressed and shaven. He took it with him to the library and then the lab, planning to conduct these experiments, and see if he could find new theories to test. He missed having lunches with Eve; she regularly met with Phillip for that meal.

Adam chuckled when she came into the room one night. "You look like you've been pinched." He sobered quickly. "He didn't, did he?" Adam had been fighting his jealousy since the first match. When he hadn't seen Phillip pursuing more than Eve's hand, he had calmed.

"He kissed me," she said in a voice that matched her wide eyes.

"Phillip?" Adam said in disbelief.

"No, Ducat Evan won tonight," she said, shaking her head very slowly.

Evan was younger, much closer to Eve's own age, and quite obviously attracted to her. Adam jumped from the bed and stalked out of the room; Eve didn't move. Adam found Bianca just entering the suite.

"How long?" he asked his mother.

"I'm afraid I need more information than that," she said snidely.

"How long until I'm allowed to play for her affection?" he asked.

Bianca laughed. "You have her affection, you fool. If you didn't, would you still be sleeping in her bed?"

"You know we aren't that intimate, right?" he verified. "We share the bed."

Bianca laughed again. "I know, and you can justify it how you like. She wouldn't have Evan sharing her bed though; I can assure you of that."

"You can?" he asked.

"You can be slow-witted sometimes, Adam. Go, sleep. Let her shave you again in the morning, and then see if you still doubt."

Betty had resumed shaving duties after Adam and Eve had been late two mornings in a row. Adam considered this.

"How long?" he asked again.

"Well, you should really let as many of them as wish to have their try. Unless you are quite sure of your abilities. I doubt you want to give up your suit."

He grumbled. He did not like this situation, not at all.

Eve had changed and was tightly curled under the covers when he returned. He didn't get in right away, instead coming to her side of the bed and smoothing her hair from her face.

"Don't be afraid. You are your own," he reminded her.

She took a shaky breath and relaxed. "Right, and if I ask him not to kiss me again, he won't, right?"

Adam closed his eyes and balled his fists. "Right." His voice was hard. She shivered a little and ducked more of her face under her blanket. Things were not going to get easier soon.

*

Evan did not meet Eve for lunch, but he did walk her to her rooms again after his next win. His kisses made their way up her arm. Eve was relieved when Mother approached behind him, and he was obligated to release her. She tried not to feel claimed. The decision was still hers in the end.

Evan continued to court Eve's attentions. He invited her to lunch with him in his suite, as well. He had no family to share with, so his rooms were very small. Eve felt a little uncomfortable alone with him. He wasn't as good at initiating conversation as Phillip had been, seemingly more interested in watching her than listening to her. She finally extricated herself, claiming she wished to bathe before her afternoon meeting.

Eve found Mother and excused herself from the afternoon. She was too frazzled to be of assistance to Her. The High One hoped she would enjoy her bath and told her not to worry about the meeting. Eve went alone to the baths and felt better as soon as she was surrounded by the warm water. She sighed and closed her eyes.

"What have we here?" She recognized that voice, but hadn't heard it in weeks. She looked over her shoulder to see Louis, naked, leering at her. She hadn't thought of him as 'Prince' since his assault outside the hall. She groaned and sank again in her tub.

He stepped to the foot of her bath and held her eyes. "I understand you are still on Evan's hand. Has he been using those hands well?" he asked, touching her foot where it was on the edge of the tub.

She pulled it back into the water and sat up a little. "I was told we didn't linger outside the baths."

Louis laughed. "True. Can I share yours?"

He moved to the next tub, which a servant was just filling with water. He climbed in.

"So, Eve." She shuddered at him using her name. She almost preferred he call her 'Server girl'. "How are you going to choose in the end? Are you actually going to marry the winner?"

"I'm not sure. Probably," Eve wondered why he was asking but continued with her answer. "I don't have another way of choosing at the moment. I certainly appreciate intelligence. A husband with a solid mind would be a good match."

Louis looked at her again. At least he couldn't look into her tub any longer.

"And you think *Adam*," he said the word like it was offensive, "has a solid mind? Perhaps, rocks for brains," he muttered.

Eve rolled her eyes and shook her head. "And the vastly witty Prince who slept through Ernst Peter's class is going to prove more intelligent?" she mocked.

"Indeed," he said quietly.

She didn't want to get out of the tub while he was there, but at least he was safely in a tub of his own. Eve motioned for a servant to bring a towel and rose from her bath. She quickly wrapped the towel around herself, affording Louis as little time to see her as she could manage.

He grabbed her hand as she passed. "My attentions haven't wandered," he reminded her, as she shuddered.

That evening, Evan lost to a Prince, Jasper. Jasper was tall, slender, and very fair-haired. He almost looked grey, but he wasn't as old as that. He kissed her hand, but did not make any other show of affection. He didn't walk her to her rooms or ask her to lunch. She smiled as he left and stayed with Mother as She tended the boards.

"Jasper doesn't show his emotions. He is quite secretive," She told Eve. "He was hurt by a woman in the past and prefers to keep himself aloof."

Eve nodded. She would be careful to ensure Jasper knew she was looking for honour, not love. In truth, she wasn't looking for either; not holding value in the first and having already found the second.

"You are later than usual," Adam complained. "Did Evan keep you occupied?"

Eve laughed. "No, I stayed with Mother. Prince Jasper defeated him tonight."

"Jasper?" he asked. "I didn't think he was looking for a wife."

Eve changed behind the door again. "Well, perhaps he has changed his mind. Mother said he was hurt in the past?" She came out and tucked herself into Adam's side.

Adam put his arm around Eve. "Yes, she decided to leave on the results of a match, but they were closer than name alone. That's why I'm surprised he is looking to marry again."

"Well," she said as she yawned, "we'll see what comes." She put her head on his chest. "I still want you," she murmured as her eyes closed.

Adam beamed and kissed her head. "I want you too."

Jasper was challenged twice over the next week. It seemed her suitors were finally dwindling. Jasper was a competent player and won both matches. He still didn't say much to her, merely taking her hand again after each one.

"You play very well," she complimented him after his third win. He still hadn't spoken to her.

"I have had to learn quickly." His voice was deep.

His eyes met hers for the first time. She could see herself respecting and admiring this man. There was strength in his face, in his manner.

When she didn't add anything else, he kissed her hand again and left.

"You got him to speak." Mother seemed surprised.

"So it seems." Eve left Mother with the boards and followed the Prince out of the hall. She didn't see him in the atrium; he must walk quickly. She started to head for her room.

"Eve." She closed her eyes. *Not Louis, not at night, not alone.*

She turned to face him. He held a pink crystal in his hand. "This is for you. I don't know that I will defeat Jasper tomorrow, but I want you to have it anyway."

Eve held out her hand, and Louis dropped the bloom there. He closed her fingers over it and pulled her to him. She fought the urge to turn and run. He hadn't done anything deserving such a rude response. Well, not tonight, at any rate.

"I hope you won't let past transgressions bear on your decision." He kissed her cheek and left.

Eve felt her stomach flop. She wasn't sure if she should be sickened or relieved. He hadn't tried anything improper, but he was still pursuing her. She felt a pain in her hand and realized she was clenching the bloom. Sighing, she opened her hand to see it. It was carved from quartz crystal and was very finely done. Mother found her still standing there looking at it.

"Who is that from?" she asked.

"Prince Louis."

"Really. Well, it is quite lovely." Bianca started to walk down the hall but stopped when She didn't hear Eve following. She grabbed Eve's arm and pulled her along beside Her. "Are you well?" She asked.

"He, he tormented me when I was a Server, and he came after me once, weeks ago. I just... don't know what to make of it."

"Well, he has to defeat Jasper before you need to think on it at all."

Eve nodded. Jasper was a very good player; this might still amount to nothing. She tucked the bloom away before entering her room.

Adam still noticed something was wrong. "Did Jasper lose?" he asked while she changed.

"No. He – he plays very well," she said.

"Then what is the matter, Eve?"

"Louis," she whispered, holding onto Adam. She shivered.

"What did he do now?" he asked.

"Nothing, wrong, just... he is going to challenge tomorrow." Eve shivered again.

"Don't worry about it. You know he won't win." Adam kissed her, rubbing his hands up and down her cold arms.

"Right." She tried to be confident, but she wasn't sure. She kissed Adam again, looking for some peace to help her sleep. She wrapped her arms around his waist and pulled him closer, wishing she could crawl right inside him. He made her feel safe.

"Eve? Are you sure it isn't more?" he asked her when the kiss broke. He stroked her cheek lightly.

"Make me forget?" she pleaded.

He chuckled, "Forget he exists? Happily." He kissed her again, deeply, and pulled one of her legs over his, running his hand along its length.

She gasped, "Yes, thank you." She kissed him again and let the blissful feelings carry her away.

*

Adam felt Eve's weight shift slightly, and he began stroking her back. "I was wondering if you were going to wake up soon," he teased.

Eve started. "Am I late?" She snapped to attention.

He chuckled. "No, not really. Betty will have you ready in plenty of time. Mother is taking the morning off. She's going for a ride and then to the baths. If you're going to join her, you will need to dress. If you'd rather stay with me..." He pulled her closer, making his preference known. He'd gotten to spend noon time with her of late, but nothing outside that. He was dearly hoping she'd stay at his side for the morning.

She settled back into his arms. "Well, in that case." She nuzzled her nose in his chest hair.

“Still not over that, are you?” he said with a laugh.

“I told you. I’ve never seen any before.” Her fascination had been found out pretty quickly.

“I can’t believe how easy it is to just be here with you.” He pulled her into a tighter embrace. “I thought it would be hard to be so close, but it isn’t.” He kissed her forehead. He thought he would be awake every night, resisting the urge to press himself on her, but it hadn’t been like that. Well, it had last night, but that was his own fault. Normally, it was a comfort to sleep with her smell filling his nose, her even breathing in his ears.

She giggled. “You tickle.”

“Time for a shave?” he asked lustfully.

She blushed and laughed, “I suppose it is.”

Betty was waiting for them in the sitting room. She uncovered their breakfasts. Then, she set the shaving supplies at Eve’s side and excused herself with a large grin on her face.

Eve blushed again. “When did she stop being discreet?”

“The first morning I wasn’t in the closet,” Adam muttered, sipping his tea.

“Really?” Eve asked, breaking open her biscuit.

“Yes, you didn’t notice? It was worse when she took over shaving.” There was something in Betty’s demeanour screaming ‘you can’t handle it,’ which was all the worse because it was true.

“No. I guess I got distracted around then.” She frowned. “What am I going to do, Adam? I don’t *want* to marry Jasper.” She put her head in her hands. She took a deep breath and shook herself once before she started on her breakfast. Adam noticed how quickly she changed her posture, as though she simply shook off the troubling thought.

He grabbed her wrist. “Don’t worry too much about it, all right? I still have a match to play, remember?”

She bent to kiss him before grabbing the lather. “I didn’t. Thank you for reminding me.”

The shave took especially long this morning. Adam was constantly interrupting Eve, making her jump as his hands wandered.

"You should be more careful when a woman is holding a knife," she scolded him.

He took a deep breath and calmed himself. "Right you are." He grinned madly.

"Tell me what you've been making in the lab," she requested, shaving him efficiently now that he held still.

"A little of this, a little of that."

She wiped the blade and tapped it on her hand menacingly.

"All right," he chuckled. "Don't hurt me. We made salt. Good salt. We've also found a way to make more acid from sulphur. That's what you did that first day, by the way."

"Really?" she asked, removing the last of the lather. "A sulphuric acid?"

He pulled her into his lap and put his face near hers. "Precisely." He kissed her, then took the knife from her hand and dropped it on the table.

Adam kissed her again, taking his time to enjoy every inch of her lips.

"And what did you do with this acid?" she asked when he let her go for air.

"We etched glass. It was fascinating. It left the surface clouded, almost like it was covered in frost, but more regular."

Eve blinked then. She pushed herself up and went to her room for a moment. "Like this?" she asked, holding out a pink crystal bloom with rough surfaces.

"Where did you...?" Adam started to ask, but then took it from her. "Yes, just like this; but who?"

"Louis," she breathed. "Was he in the lab with you?" she asked.

"No, not then. He was other days." Adam shifted awkwardly in his chair, remembering the torment the lout had given him, talking of Eve's suitors.

"I thought he'd carved it, but after hearing you describe the effects... Sand is quartz, as well; that's why it would work on this as well as glass."

"I didn't know that," Adam murmured, still looking over the favour. Why was Louis giving her favours at all? He finally handed it back to her. "What are you going to do?"

She burst into tears. "That's what I asked you!" She quickly sniffed and stood up, pushing her fear away. Her pain tore into his heart.

Adam wrapped his arms around her shoulders and chest, pulling her back against him. "I'm sorry. I know this is hard for you. I didn't expect this," he said, looking back at the bloom on the table. "I thought he was just hounding you."

"So did I," she whispered. "He asked me the other day if I was going to marry the winner. I didn't think anything of it at the time. I didn't think he stood a chance of winning." She looked back at the etched quartz. He was brighter than either of them had given him credit for. "He is jealous of you," she murmured, putting her face into his chest again as she turned.

"He should be," Adam told her. "I have the best thing in the world. When did you talk to him? You never mentioned it."

Eve grimaced slightly, "It was after my lunch with Evan. I went to the baths, and he found me there."

Adam's hands tightened reflexively and Eve winced slightly. "I'm sorry," he apologized, loosening his grip. "Baths, eh? Well, Mother will be headed there after her ride. Shall we?" he asked.

"That would be lovely," Eve said. She headed for the room to change. She was about to step behind the door when she laughed and pulled the gown over her head.

Adam froze, seeing her pale skin, flawless, down her back. He couldn't stop staring, swallowing hard.

"Well, you're going to see me in the bath anyway," she reminded him, pulling out the plainest of her dresses.

"Right," he said, stepping forward to tear his eyes from her. He found his own clothes, careful not to look too closely at her until she had the dress on. He still turned away to change. His interest would be obvious when they got to the baths, unless he got it under control by then; he was going to try. Eve sat on the bed, waiting for him.

Adam was successful in calming himself by the time they reached the baths. He was just overly conscious of Eve, that's all. Being in the bath made everything simpler. He was accustomed to nakedness here and stripped down quickly. Eve didn't join him.

"Something wrong?" he asked, his hands still at the waist of his pants.

"He's here," she whispered.

"It's all right. Don't run away from him." Adam held her eyes while he opened her robe.

She took a deep breath and finished on her own. He held her hand, leading her to the tubs. Adam looked to Louis. He appeared to be simply soaking; he hadn't noticed them yet. The servant had begun filling the tub beside him. Adam moved to take it.

"Adam," Louis said coolly. "Eve," he smiled.

Eve nodded to him briefly, waiting for the servant to fill the tub. "Here, take this one," Adam muttered, wanting her in the water and out of Louis' line of sight.

Eve sank into the warm water with a clenched jaw.

"So, Louis, I heard you found another use for Derek's acid," Adam said snidely.

"Oh, did Eve show you my favour?" he asked, leaning over the edge of his tub. He smiled at her again. Adam fought the raging jealousy that struck him. "I'm glad you liked it," he said to her. "Yes, it worked well on the quartz. It took a few tries to work out how to shape crevices, but it turned out nicely, I think." Indeed, it was a beautiful gift. Adam only wished it hadn't come from someone like Louis.

Grinding his teeth, Adam watched Eve hug her knees in her tub. Louis sighed and stretched his feet over the edge of his tub. He looked over at the other two.

"Why so glum? And why are you huddling, Eve? Isn't the water warm enough?" He waved the servant over.

"No, it's fine," she said, closing her eyes and uncurling slightly.

Adam glared at Louis over Eve's tub. She looked like she was finally easing up. He leaned back in his tub now and tried to do the same.

Louis chuckled once. "Well, I guess I'll be about my morning."

Eve flinched at his voice.

"I'm hoping to make a mount for your favour this afternoon, Eve. You won't mind me borrowing it again to put them together, will you?" he asked. A mount? So she'd be able to wear it, of course. Adam swallowed down the lump in his throat and fought his instincts.

Eve crossed her hands over her breasts. "No, that will be fine. I'll bring it to dinner tonight?" she asked. She looked to him now. Adam wondered what she saw. He was easily as tall as Adam, with dirty blonde hair. He had beady eyes, did she notice those? She must, they were trained on hers. Adam took some comfort in that. At least he wasn't leering.

"That would be perfect," he agreed. "May I?" he asked, putting his hand over her tub. She stared up at him, wide-eyed.

Adam stood and got out of his tub. It was too much, his reaching for her. He would touch her in the baths? "You press the limit of propriety," he fumed.

Louis rolled his eyes. "I only wanted her hand." He brushed the back of his hand against her cheek, instead, as he walked away.

Eve sank right under the water. She was uncomfortable. Adam wasn't helping. He was ready to chew through the tub; he wouldn't be any comfort to her now.

He followed Louis, "You can't think you'll ever actually win her heart."

"We'll see what I can win," Louis said over his shoulder as he left.

*

Eve sank down under the water. She didn't want to see either of them right now. She rose with a gasp moments later.

"Eve?" Mother asked, stepping into the tub Louis had vacated. "More water, please," she called. "How long was he in here?" she asked of no one in particular. Eve looked over her other shoulder, but Adam was also gone. She sighed in relief.

"Are you quite well?" Mother asked again. "Adam seemed out of sorts as he left, as well."

"Louis is planning to challenge for me tonight. He gave me that favour," Eve explained.

"Ah, I see. Jealous, is he?"

"Both of them, I think. How tied am I to the results in the hall?" she asked. "Will I be lowering myself if I don't accept the final victor?"

Mother took a moment before answering. "Not lowered, no. It would be confusing to the assembled if, after all of this time, you didn't abide by it."

Eve nodded and sighed. "Thank you, Mother." She got out of the tub.

Adam was absent at lunch. Eve showed Mother her new favour again, explaining the etching.

"Very nice," she admired, taking it into her hands. "You really do bring out the imagination in our young men, don't you?" She smiled.

"I'm worried, Mother. What if Louis wins tonight? What if Adam isn't able to defeat him?"

"Don't fret about that. What you and Adam have is strong enough to get through this, even if you do marry Louis. Trust me, I know," she smiled at Eve. "You recall my husband had another wife? Adam won't give up easily."

Eve straightened in her chair. "Right, and you have taught him how to play well. I have nothing to fear."

"Exactly. Now, are you sure you're ready to meet with Ducat Clarence? I really want you present at this meeting. Your insight into the tensions in Augustia was spot on in the last meeting. I want you as sharp today."

Eve smiled broadly and regarded Mother with her green eyes. "It is an honour and a privilege."

Ducat Clarence had much information regarding the hostilities. The situation had worsened.

"The common class is no longer willing to accept the decrees from the elite. They believe they have enough knowledge to choose their own course."

Eve could understand their viewpoint. However, a country needed a head; with everyone choosing for himself, the system broke down. It would be only a matter of time before that became evident to the citizens, and they set up a new form of governance or returned to the old.

"Have the common class appointed any leaders for themselves?" Eve asked. "A speaker for them?"

"They have not. They have a council, a group of six that have been meeting with some of the elite."

"I see, and these six, do the other commoners accept their decisions?"

"Yes, not explicitly, but generally."

"And have the elite of Augustia considered making these six elite? Ernsts perhaps?"

"I don't know that they have. You think the common would accept the rest of the rule if they had more input into the process?"

Eve nodded. "A good suggestion, but I would not be the one to make it. Perhaps Vanto Albert?"

"Perhaps Eve herself," the High One suggested.

Eve looked to her, wide-eyed. "I – I would be honoured."

"I won't send you off immediately, Eve." Mother smiled. "Take some time with Clarence and Albert. They can prepare you for what you will be facing."

Clarence nodded, "Indeed. I can give you the names and descriptions of the Most High of Augustia. I can also give you the names of the six. Vanto Albert would be a better instructor for conduct within Augustia. I spend most of my time in the lesser circles."

Eve nodded, still overwhelmed. "I would appreciate your assistance and instruction."

"Excellent. Clarence, please write up what you can for Eve so that she might have time to prepare herself."

He nodded, and Bianca dismissed him.

"You are sure you are up for this?" Bianca asked Eve.

"No, but I am willing to try. I think I will be, after preparation."

Mother smiled at her. "Wonderful. Come, let's prepare for dinner."

*

Adam was in Eve's room when she came to find evening attire. He was already dressed in her favourite blue jacket and scarlet pants. He needed time to digest what he had learned this afternoon. He looked to her as she crossed to the wardrobe.

"Perhaps I shall match you tonight," she said with a smile, pulling out the deep blue gown and red robe. He tried to smile in return, but it slipped.

She pulled her robe off, still speaking, "You left the bath quickly. Is everything fine?"

He sat on the bed heavily. He had disappeared into the lab, hoping to find what Louis was making her; it was a ring. He was going to put that bloom on her finger. Even simpler for her to keep on her person than his own. Louis had also forged some alloy of copper and gold that was a lovely pink shade.

"Adam?" she asked now. He looked up; she was undressed, but the worry creasing her brow kept his eyes on her face. "What is wrong?" she asked, taking a seat beside him.

"You should dress." He looked away. He did not want to leer, or offend her. If he started looking, he wouldn't be able to stop.

"Of course," she said, rising. Louis was going to play for her tonight. He was going to put that ring on her finger. He was sure of it. She pulled on her gown and robe and returned to his side, dressed. "Will you tell me now?"

He cupped her cheek. "The same as earlier, worrying over nothing. You should go to Betty, finish getting ready."

"Very well." She kissed him on the cheek. "Please don't fret. Mother made me feel better this afternoon. You should talk with Her." Adam could hear how she still put the honorific in her references to Mother.

"That is a good idea," he agreed, and followed her from the room.

Adam sat on his mother's bed while Eve was being painted for dinner. "What do I do?"

"Adam, I know I seem to be able to read your mind, but I actually can't. What are you talking about?" she asked.

"We're close, but if this goes badly... Is it better that I take my chance now, or wait until it has played out? What if I never have her to myself again?"

Bianca laughed. "Is that what you are worried about? You are as silly as she is. If you love her... You do love her, don't you?" she verified. Adam nodded solemnly. "Then it won't matter what comes. You will win her back if you lose her the first; just as I won Richard from Vicky. You won't let it stop you."

"But if I forfeit my attentions, how can I win her back?"

Bianca paused, considering this. “There is always a way. Perhaps she will just have to *lose* her husband. It has been done, but it is not wise.”

Adam put his head in his hands. Mother’s advice had not comforted him as much as he’d hoped.

“The best plan is to not lose in the first place,” she said with a laugh. “I know you’ve only played once, but you played very well. I’m sure there will be no trouble at all.”

“Thank you, Mother.” If Bianca told him he played well, he trusted her judgement. He hugged her before returning to Eve in the suite.

*

Eve looked to Adam as he entered. Had Mother been able to ease his mind? It seemed so; he appeared to be in better spirits. He even came and kissed her. “Better?” she asked.

“Better,” he answered.

Eve tucked the quartz flower into her pocket and took Adam’s arm.

Prince Jasper was unsurprised when Louis came to challenge him. Eve joined them at the Cargon table. She was terribly interested in the outcome of this particular match.

“Did you bring it, Most High?” Louis asked when she approached.

“Yes.” She pulled the bloom from her pocket.

He plucked it from her hand gently. “Excellent. I will have it back to you at dinner tomorrow night. I should have waited to give it to you, but I couldn’t. May I check the fit?” he asked, producing the band.

He slid it onto one of her fingers. “Excellent,” he murmured and kissed her hand.

“Your move,” Jasper said coldly.

“Yes, right.” Louis turned back to the boards now. Eve moved to Jasper’s side to watch the game progress. He looked to her once or twice, surprised to have her there. She usually sat until the end of the game.

"Concerned?" he asked at one point.

"Yes. I do not want him to win."

Jasper chuckled, and it sounded very odd, as though he hadn't done so in a long time. "I don't either."

She looked to him now. She had been careful not to give him any indication that her interest went further than the moment. Folding her arms across her chest, she rubbed her arms. She needed to relax. The world changed based on the outcome of the Game, but this would not be the last Game played.

Jasper shrugged out of his coat and slid it onto her shoulders. She met his eyes again and he smiled at her. "You looked cold," he commented.

"I was, thank you." She looked at the board again. Jasper was lined up to make several attacks if Louis stepped wrongly. Louis, however, had set his defence very carefully and had several options open to him. She shivered despite the jacket Jasper had so kindly given her. She looked across the board and noticed a twist to Louis' lips. He was looking at the jacket in distaste. When he noticed her looking, he changed the intent of his gaze. She knew he was removing more than just the jacket in his mind.

Eve pulled the jacket tighter around her and made a point of breathing deeply from the fabric. If jealousy made him err, that would suit her. She also took a step closer to Jasper. He eyed her for a moment before turning his attention back to the board.

The hall was beginning to clear. Mother came to stand with Eve and Jasper.

"Interesting," she murmured, looking at both the board and Eve's jacket.

Eve pulled up the jacket and hid her face in it. Louis looked angry again. She kept her face hidden so he wouldn't see her smirk. She did enjoy irritating him as he tormented her. Adam took a place behind Louis and smiled at Eve, winking.

Each player was taking longer and longer between moves. Eve yawned in spite of herself. Jasper looked to her again, then to Louis. "Can we finish this tomorrow?"

Louis looked to Eve now. "That would be fine. Then when I win, I can present your finished gift," he said to Eve.

Eve nodded to him, hoping he would depart. "How I loathe him," she muttered. She pulled off Jasper's jacket to return to him.

"Allow me to walk you to your suite?" he asked, pulling the jacket back on.

"I would like that, thank you," she said, taking his arm.

"Why does he seek you so doggedly?" Jasper asked. "I don't recall any of the others finding special favours. Though I see you have another," he indicated her pin.

"Yes, well, this one is from Adam," she smiled.

Jasper nodded, "Of course. You know I would not come between the two of you."

"I do, and I thank you for that. Louis would," she said coldly. She stood on her toes to kiss his cheek. She still only hit his jaw. Giggling a little, she rocked back onto her heels. "Good luck tomorrow night."

He kissed her forehead. "Sleep well," he wished her. Adam and Mother came up behind her.

"Is everything all right?" Mother asked, looking to Jasper who was just leaving.

"What fool woman let him go?" Eve wondered aloud.

Mother laughed, "A fool indeed. She has been passed more than once since then. She should have kept her eyes on her heart instead of her status."

Adam took Eve's hand, leading her to the bedroom.

"Adam?" she asked as he undressed. She hadn't begun yet. "Would you rather I change behind the door?"

He hung his head and pulled his loose pants on. "No," he said quietly.

"You're certain?" she asked again. His tone certainly hadn't reassured her.

He chuckled. "I'm a little troubled by how easily you arouse me, Eve. That's why I have been... distant?"

She closed her eyes and smiled. That was why, not that she was unappealing. She hung up her robe and took off her gown. She pulled down her nightdress and felt his eyes on her. Smiling again, she pulled her hair over her shoulders to cover herself a little and turned to face him, gown in hand. It was a tiny test.

He was staring at her. He was aroused; he did desire her. She felt the flush spreading through her. "Come here," he called and she complied. "Did you think I didn't *want* to look at you?"

She looked at her toes for a second. "Yes," she admitted sheepishly.

He laughed loudly now. "How to convince you?" He let his hands slip around her bare waist and pulled her closer.

"I think you already have," she told him with a kiss. "Do you think I need this?" She tossed the nightdress on the bed beside him.

"Yes. I don't trust myself that far," he said with a laugh. "Unless you're feeling a lot bolder?" He circled his fingers on the small of her back.

She kissed him again before pulling the dress on. "Not quite as bold as that." A small laugh escaped her lips.

CHAPTER EIGHT

Eve eased herself out of Adam's arms, trying not to wake him. He rolled over, and she assumed she had succeeded. She tiptoed out of the room and sat to breakfast.

"He is still asleep?" Mother asked.

"Yes," Eve said, sipping her freshly poured tea. "I think he didn't sleep much last night," she said with a sly smile.

"I see, but you did?" Mother raised an eyebrow.

"I slept, enough." It was fun to let the women fill in the gaps in her statements. Indeed, both of them laughed now, and Eve smiled, too.

The morning passed uneventfully, but there was a knock on the door of the suite while Eve and Mother were at lunch. At the High One's nod, Betty opened the door.

"Prince Jasper," Eve said happily. "Please, come in. Join us."

"Thank you, Most High. I was actually just passing through. I wanted to give you this."

Eve came to the door to accept his gift. It was a paper flower, folded from pink pages. Eve giggled a little as she took it gently. "This is wonderful. Thank you." She pulled him down a little so she could actually reach his cheek this time.

"Your smile is infectious, Most High," he sighed. "I'll leave you to your meal."

"You are sure you won't stay?" Eve asked again.

"Thank you, no." He turned to leave.

Eve frowned as she came back to the table, setting the bloom safely away from the food. She smiled again when she looked on it.

"He's right. You are infectious," Mother murmured. "You've brought laughter back to this suite. You've roused elite into actions they wouldn't have considered before, and I hear the lab is positively bubbling with activity stemming from your notes. Adam should really return those to you."

"Pebbles in the sea," Eve whispered with a dreamy look. "Why wouldn't he stay?" Perhaps Mother would know the reason.

"I think he's concerned he's becoming attached to you. You are obviously with Adam, and he has no intention of intruding on that. At the same time, I think he would very much like to have you in his life. When you've been hurt, building any attachment can be painful."

Eve nodded. "I would like to get to know him better."

"You would be one of very few if you did, Eve," Mother smiled.

*

Eve had changed for dinner before Adam returned from the lab. She was sitting with Mother when he did come in. He stormed past them.

"What's the matter, Adam?" she asked.

He just shook his head and started unbuttoning his jacket on the way to their room. He threw it onto the bed and yanked his shirt over his head. He heard stitches tear and couldn't care less.

"Adam?" Eve asked from behind him. He turned to her, his shirt in hand. He was shaking. "What is it?"

What was it? It was Louis, as always -- his vile language, his licentious thoughts. Having seen her in the bath, he was able to describe her far too well. The rage was nearly beyond his control.

"You know. You've heard it before. I've never had to listen to it, though." He threw the shirt into the wardrobe and grabbed her to him roughly. He needed to touch her, remind himself that she was here, that she wanted to be here. She was a little startled, but craned her neck to look up at him. "Louis was describing what he wants to do with you when you are his." The shaking became worse.

"Ah," she said. "He isn't often vocal, but I have an idea." She gripped his chin and pulled it down. She kissed him.

Adam sighed. She didn't need this; she didn't need to see him in pieces.

"I'm sorry, Eve. It was... very difficult to hear."

"I understand. He is never going to *have* me," she reminded him. "Even if he wins, even if I feel obligated to marry him, he will have my hand only. You will always have my heart."

"And he isn't going to win," Adam reminded them both. He kissed her again, more gently now. "I love you."

"I know, and I love you."

Adam walked her to the High Table and left her at Mother's side, then moved back to his table. There was a note by his plate.

The Server girl's smell is divine. I'm sure her taste is even sweeter.

It wasn't signed, but Adam didn't need it to be. He crumpled the paper in his hand. He heard a bark of a laugh from one of the lower tables.

Martina came to his side. "May I sit with you, cousin?" she asked. He hadn't realized she was attending dinner. His cousin was only sixteen.

Adam took a deep breath and smiled at her. "That would be lovely. Did Aunt Maria send you?" he asked.

Martina chuckled. “Your distress is not well hidden, Adam. Are you troubled about the matches?” She sipped her wine carefully. “I heard Jasper was a very good player. Are you concerned you will lose to him?”

“Not him, no. I don’t even know that I’d challenge him. He is a good husband for Eve and would respect our relationship. It’s his current challenger that has me at my wit’s end.”

“Ah, yes, Louis. There is much talk of him among the women.”

That caught Adam’s attention. “How so?”

“He is a cad. He has been in many rooms, and most reports are positive. Apparently, he has been absent of late, and some are wondering if it is because he has his eyes on a particular prize.”

Adam clenched his jaw.

“Adam. She is not like them. You know that. I’ve seen how she looks at you. She isn’t looking for a brief night of bliss, she wants to keep you.”

“How is it you can talk of these things and I don’t feel like I’m going to ignite from the heat of my own skin? My mother says one word, and I think I’m going to die.”

Martina laughed, “That’s easy, because you are her child, and you see her from that position. I’m your cousin; we are of an age. Well, nearly.” She was only a handful of years younger than Adam. Vast when they were young, not nearly so much any longer. “If you are embarrassed, it’s for me, that I have this knowledge at all.”

He laughed now. “You are right there. I hope you aren’t taking up with cads like Louis,” he warned.

“Hardly,” she chuckled. “I’m to be with Douglas, and we are getting along quite well. I don’t see any reason to go looking for some time.”

Adam shook his head. “When did you grow up?”

She laughed more loudly. “When you were busy in meetings with the High One, when James and Delilah drove me to grey hair.

I'm not kidding, look." She pulled a few strands over her shoulder; there were shots of white in it.

Adam shook his head. She swatted him.

"James did it – brought a compound back from the lab and doused my hair while I slept. He won't be laughing when he finds the frogs I've hidden under his bed. They should be getting out about now. I didn't tie the lid to the box."

Adam laughed louder. It stopped abruptly as Jasper and Louis rose.

"Time already?" Martina mused. "You will be staying, I presume?" she asked as her dessert dish was taken. Adam nodded. "Well, I wish you all the best, cousin." She kissed his cheek and followed her parents from the hall.

*

Eve moved to Jasper's side. "Thank you again."

He smiled at her and took her hand. "My pleasure."

Louis' eyes narrowed as he moved. Eve glared at the board. It was nearing the end now. There were fewer and fewer safe plays. She tried to count moves to see who would win.

Louis pulled the ring from his pocket and set it on the Cargon table in front of him. Eve refused to look at it, keeping her eyes locked on the board.

Jasper took her hand again. "I am sorry, Second. It seems I have to disappoint you." Eve looked up at him, eyes wide. His face was filled with regret. He moved another piece and Eve counted again. He was going to lose. Her heart sank. Her knees nearly gave out. There were still a few moves. Louis might make a mistake.

Eve held her breath as the Game wound down. Adam and Mother were still in their seats, but both leaned forward. They could see it, too.

Jasper shook his head. "It seems I have not improved enough." There was no move that wouldn't open the goal for attack. Making a move regardless, he stepped back, bowed to Louis, and turned to go.

Eve turned to catch his arm, but he was already out of her reach. Louis grabbed her trailing hand and lifted it to his lips. Eve closed her eyes, not wanting to face him. She took one deep breath, gritted her teeth, and reminded herself that she would do her duty. She could not simply slight him out of hand. She was Second.

His lips were still on the back of her hand. His eyes brightened when they found hers. He produced the ring he had made and slid it slowly onto her finger. "Please, accept my favour and my offer."

She closed her eyes again, this time trying not to weep. She didn't want to accept either, but Mother was right. "Thank you," she whispered.

"May I escort you to your suite?" he asked as he reset the board.

Was there a polite way out of this? Adam was already moving to Mother's side. If they were behind her, she might be able to endure it.

"You may."

Rather than wrap her hand into his arm, Louis held it up, admiring his favour. "It looks even lovelier there," he mused.

She didn't answer, walking slowly alongside him.

"I do hope I have impressed upon you both my ability and my determination. I didn't expect it to be quite so difficult to get this close to you again, but I am glad to be so."

She pulled her hand away at the door. "Thank you, Highness. Good evening to you."

"And to you," he wished her. He bent and kissed her cheek before she had a chance to realize his intention. He left his hands at her hips. Eve looked down the hall. How far away were Mother and Adam? His fingers were stroking now.

"Good evening," she repeated and ducked through the door.

*

Adam's hand clenched on his mother's arm. "Adam, that is not untoward. She did accept his favour. It is difficult, but you must bide your time. Tomorrow." His mother's voice was soothing, but his nerves were still on fire.

Louis bowed to the High One now. "Good Evening, Most High," he bade her at the door. *Sweeter,* he mouthed to Adam once Bianca had turned to follow Eve into the suite. He licked his lips. Adam punched out reflexively. Louis caught his fist in a palm. "Accepted. Tomorrow?"

"Tomorrow," Adam whispered. He turned to see Eve in the open doorway. He looked to her hands; she had already pulled off the ring. He smiled and turned to Louis. His eyes were on her hands as well. "Excuse me, Highness." He put a hand to Eve's cheek as he stepped to her. She covered it with her own and then pulled him forward by it.

"How I loathe him," they said in unison once the door was closed.

"At least he didn't request a lunch," Eve continued. "I would have declined that offer, polite or not."

Mother shook her head. "You must report if he does anything improper, Eve. Otherwise, you should treat him as any other suitor."

"I know," she muttered. "I know." She headed for the bedroom.

Adam moved to follow, but Mother stopped him. "Tomorrow?" she asked.

Adam hung his head. He reached into a pocket and pulled out the note. "He taunted me," Adam admitted. "I shouldn't have risen to his bait."

Bianca looked at the crumpled words and her eyes blazed. "You shouldn't have, but I can't say I wouldn't have done the same. Vicky was never so... malicious."

Adam felt his mother's arms around him and hugged her back. "I'm going to beat the cretin, right?"

"Of course you are, love. Of course you are."

Adam found Eve already under the covers when he came into the room. She had changed quickly. He endeavoured to do the same.

"Adam?" Eve asked.

He slipped into the bed across from her. "Yes?"

She climbed on top of him, wrapping her arms around his chest. "I don't want to go to him." Her tears were falling onto him. "I don't want him to have anything of me."

He curled his arms around her and stroked her hair and back. "I know. I don't want that either."

Eve was very reluctant to leave Adam the next morning, lingering much longer than her itinerary would allow. She rose and dressed slowly while Adam watched her from the bed. There was nothing more he could do until tonight. He wished there were; he wished he could be at her side the whole day. She looked so fragile. She finished dressing and picked up the ring from where she had left it last night, as though it weighed many pounds.

"Come here," Adam called to her. He took the ring from her. "I love you. This," he slipped it on her finger, "is just a token. This," he put a hand to her breasts, over the copper bud, "is nothing more. This," he took her face between his hands and kissed her. "This is everything."

She smiled. "Thank you."

"Go, and don't be afraid. I will win you back tonight." He hoped he sounded more certain than he felt. She looked like she believed him. That was the important part.

While Eve spent the morning in meetings with the High One, Adam went to the library. Louis found him there. He held a book on alloys and flopped into a nearby chair. He sighed contentedly and stretched his legs out.

Adam ignored him and went back to his and Eve's notes. He was trying to use her extrapolations to make some of his own. Eve's notes were suddenly lifted from his table.

"Excuse me?" he asked Louis.

"Just wondering what you have there. Oh, not the library's, my apologies." He returned it quickly. "Wait, can I have another look at that?" He moved to Adam's side, reading over his shoulder. "Where did you get this?" He flipped the page, and Adam had to resist the urge to slap his hands away.

"My room." Adam's smile was smug.

"This isn't your writing. That is." He pointed to page Adam's pen hovered over. "This isn't ink, it's charcoal. Where did you get this?" he demanded again.

"I told you, Highness. My room." Adam's icy blue eyes met Louis' stormy grey ones.

"I'm going to enjoy having her," Louis murmured, finally catching on. "I'm going to enjoy keeping her."

"Tonight," Adam said coldly, closing the book on Louis' hand.

"Tonight."

*

Eve sat at lunch with Mother. Adam had come and gone quickly. He thanked her for her book and kissed her cheek before leaving. Eve shrugged to Mother, "I guess he found something to derive from it. He can't still be testing my theories."

"I suppose not," Mother agreed. "You had many, but not *that* many."

There was a knock on the door. Mother motioned Betty to open it.

"Prince Louis, Most High. I was wondering if I might join the Second for lunch."

Mother looked to her for an answer. Eve took a deep breath before speaking. "Of course you may. Come in, Louis." She rose to meet him at the door. "And you may call me Eve."

"Thank you, Eve." He put his hands to her waist and kissed her cheek again. Betty curtsied and left to find another plate of food. When he turned to the table, Eve met Mother's eyes. *Stay,* she mouthed. Mother nodded.

"Your suite is quite cozy, Most High. I still share with my parents. It has gotten a little crowded, as you might imagine."

"Yes, well, this is large enough for us," Eve answered. She didn't know what he was getting at.

"Just the two of you?" Ah, that's what he was referring to.

The High One answered now. "Yes. Eve's chambers and mine."

"I see," Louis answered, reaching for an empty tea cup. Eve poured for him. "Thank you, Eve."

This was far worse than lunch with Evan. Not only was Louis not trying to engage her in conversation, he was deliberately setting her on edge. Could this situation be any worse, Eve wondered. Yes, Mother might not be here. That would be infinitely worse.

"So, when Eve does marry..."

"There is only one Second," Bianca said coldly. "Unless she invites the one she marries here, he will not trespass."

"Trespass? That does not sound very... familial." He knew exactly how far he could press each of them.

Eve rose. "Excuse me." She walked to her room and closed the door behind her. Leaning against the wood, she tried to even her breathing. She was going to lose her lunch if she didn't calm herself. She spied Jasper's paper bloom; it rested beside Lane's. That sight did what her even breathing could not. She turned and opened the door again.

Mother had gone. Why? Why was he still here? Betty was in the room, but that was little help. She straightened her back and returned to the table.

Louis met her in the middle of the room. He grabbed both her hands and put them around his hips. She tried to pull back, but he had both wrists in one hand now. She glared up.

"Fair Eve. You no longer wear your first favour," he commented, running a hand through her loose hair.

"No. I do still have it," she assured him.

"Good. I told you my attention would outlast his." She tried to pull her hands back again.

"I enjoy being near you, Eve, and this token." He reached to her breasts now and she pulled harder trying to back away from him. He pulled the pin out and released her hands. She fell as her weight suddenly shifted. "This token is much more fragile than mine." He folded the bud between his hands, dropping it at her feet. Then he squatted, offering her his hand. "Mine will outlast this one, as well."

She pulled her feet under her and rose without his help. "This," she took the ring from her finger, "is only a token."

"Indeed." Louis took it from her fingers and turned it. "I had hoped you liked it. I hoped I might have made up for some of my past indiscretions. The most recent, I must apologize, come from the Vanto who would be indiscreet himself."

Eve smiled. Adam was taunting him. "The Vanto? I should inform you, I have no intentions of ceasing my relations with Vanto Adam. If that is a problem, perhaps you should rethink your suit."

"Hmm, perhaps I should. Or perhaps you should learn what you are missing." He let the threat hang for a moment. Then he pulled her to him and put his lips to hers. He released her again. "Please, keep my favour in any event." He slid it back on her finger and left the room.

Eve sank to the floor and put her face into her hands. What did he do to her? Why did he do this to her?

"Most High? Can I do anything for you? Get anything?" Betty was crouched beside her, and Eve threw her arms around Betty's neck. She fell beside Eve and patted her back. "I'm sorry I couldn't help. You will be all right. Adam will stop him."

Eve knew that Betty ceased being a servant when she was alone with Mother. She wanted the same and was glad to have it.

"He won't stop. He won't stop until he possesses me. I don't understand. Why does he want me so badly?"

"We always want what we can't have."

"Do you believe that?" Eve asked her. "I have only ever wanted what was in my reach, until I wanted out of that evil man's sight and grasp. That was something I couldn't do for myself as I was." She whimpered again. "And, apparently, I can't do it as I am, either. He will never leave me be."

"Come, Most High. The High One will be waiting for you. I'll get a damp cloth." Betty came with a wet kerchief and wiped Eve's face. She straightened Eve's hair and helped her to her feet. "Never let him see what he does to you."

Eve nodded. She couldn't let him know he had as much hold on her as he did. She went to her afternoon meeting with her head high. She would be a credit to her duty.

Adam met her as she changed for dinner. He spun her and kissed her. He then picked her up and dropped her on the bed, throwing himself atop her with a laugh.

"The power of light!" he laughed. He kissed her again. His hands roamed under her gown. She blushed and bit her lip. "You, you are brilliant," he said, kissing her again and pulling the gown off her.

"Adam!" She looked to be sure the door was closed. "We need to be at dinner."

"There is time," he complained. "You need a more festive gown anyway. The saffron coloured one. Yes, yes, the saffron. Yellow." His kisses trailed down her, and she squirmed a little, unsure where this was going. His head came back to hers, and he held her eyes as his hand caressed. "The energy moves through the acidic solution, from one metal to another. You." He kissed her again. "You gave it to me."

"Adam, you found the power of light?" Her eyes were wide and he nodded.

"But it came from your notes. You gave it to me," he repeated, sealing it with his lips.

Now she giggled and wrapped herself around him, sharing his giddiness. "That is wonderful! How are we to harness it?"

"Copper seems to work remarkably well for conducting the power."

She was removing his shirt as he spoke. "And is it plentiful?" she asked, pulling it over his head.

"Not potent, but plentiful to be sure. It seems to be in all acids. Fruits, even!"

"You used juice?" she asked, incredulous. She didn't even notice they were both naked now.

"Yes!" He kissed her again and rolled over the bed with her in his arms.

There was a knock on the chamber door. "You have a challenge to honour, son. You had best be dressing."

"We will not be late, Mother!" he yelled. He kissed Eve again. "The saffron."

"Yellow," she agreed with a smile, jumping up to get it.

Eve's bubbly mood carried her out to Betty's chair.

Mother eyed Adam. "You seem to be in better spirits."

"Do I?" His grin was wide. "That would be because I had a very productive afternoon."

"And are you going to share?" She asked, shaking Her head.

"Not until I do some more testing. I also want to put that Prince out of Eve's life once and for all." His eyes blazed now. He had new confidence, new power.

Eve put her hand to Adam's arm. He opened the door to the suite and she groaned quietly. She quickly changed it to a tight smile. "Louis. You were hoping to escort me?"

"Yes, Eve. May I?" He held out his hand to her.

She took another breath before extending hers. He made a point of fondling his ring, then kissed the back of her hand before putting it to his arm. She didn't grimace or groan. She didn't smile either.

Adam extended his arm to his mother. “Thank you,” she murmured, taking it. “Will you be kind enough to wait until after the second course?” she requested. “You should eat something,” she muttered.

“Of course, Mother. I will wait until dessert is served.” He would still have plenty of time to trounce this Prince.

“That colour looks amazing on you, Eve,” Louis said, inclining his head to hers.

“Thank you. You look fine tonight as well.” He wore an appealing shade of green.

He patted her hand on his arm and chuckled.

“Something humorous?” she asked.

“Not really. That Vanto of yours, he flaunts his relation to you.”

“He is my brother,” she reminded him. Adam’s relation to her did extend past her room.

“Ah, yes,” he said, smirking even more broadly. “Close family.”

Eve ground her teeth now. Thankfully, they were at the hall.

“You are ready?” Mother asked Eve.

“Not at all. But I want this over with.”

Dessert had just been served when Adam rose and approached the smirking Louis. “I believe you already accepted my challenge,” he said before turning to the Cargon table.

Eve’s stomach flopped. She was glad she hadn’t eaten. She noticed several women looking to her now. Why? She didn’t give them much mind, focusing on the game. Adam was opening slowly, deliberating. He was setting his strategy early. Louis was playing quickly, using the same opening he had against Jasper. Adam had watched that game; surely he knew how to disrupt Louis’ attack.

“He is foolish to use the same strategy twice,” Mother agreed. “Adam is going to decimate him.”

Eve took a swallow from her red wine. Her nerves were frayed. She needed this to go correctly. Adam took more and more time with each subsequent move. People were already finishing dessert and filing out. Adam's cousin, Martina, came to the High Table. "He's going to win, Eve. You look worried, don't be."

"Thank you, Martina." Eve squeezed her hand before she left.

Some of the other Vinca seemed to take Martina's approach as an invitation. Della came. "So, you're the one who has taken Louis' attentions. I do hope you enjoy him while you can."

Eve looked to Mother with an eyebrow raised. "What was that?" Mother shook her head, and another Vinca came with a similar message.

"I knew it must be a pretty one to snag Louis from me. I'm sure he will return."

The third hoped she could handle him. "You seem too young to properly appreciate him."

"I'm surprised you made it to dinner at all," the fourth said with a smirk.

Eve rose after that to escape any others and went to stand by Louis. "Your admirers seem to think they need to inform me of what I'm missing," she whispered. Adam's eyes blazed. She met them with only slightly less fury in her own. "Do you ever sleep in your own bed?" she questioned now.

"Of late," he answered with a smile, making another move. "It has been a nice change of pace."

Eve closed her eyes and stepped a little further from him. She looked to the board again. Adam had already interrupted Louis' strategy, but he was quickly adapting it. It was very offensive. Adam had learned from Albert, it was obvious. His defence was well planned, but he would need to prepare the offence before he found himself in the same scenario as Jasper.

The turns took longer and longer. Eve did not want to spend another day on Louis' arm, but Adam would falter if he played too late into the night. She couldn't let him risk that. She looked to him, pleadingly. He could adjourn; she could give him some advice. He didn't really need it, but it would be good to talk to him about the match.

*

Adam looked to Louis. He had the same smirk on his face as last night. Eve was standing next to him. He longed to have her beside him, but here she couldn't show her true feelings, she was bound to treat him as she had every suitor before. He tried not to be distracted. She stood apart from him. It was obvious to Adam that she wanted to be on this side of the table.

What was the look on her face now? She seemed saddened, distressed. Mother came to stand by him. The hall was nearly empty. Adam looked to Eve again. His favour wasn't pinned to her gown. He stepped back, suddenly as distressed as she looked. Why had she removed it? He needed to ask her. He couldn't do that here.

"I – I think I shall have to adjourn, Highness." He bowed his head and turned quickly.

*

There was something terrible in Adam's tone. Something was wrong. Eve scrutinized the board again. It wasn't the game. It was still either player's; they'd barely passed the midpoint.

"I would appreciate the honour of escorting you again." Louis extended his hand.

Eve saw Mother leave ahead of them. She was already in the atrium. Eve turned to Louis now. "Why? Why me?"

"Why not you?" he asked. "I have been denied nothing, until now." He kissed her hand. "Nothing I wanted." He turned it and kissed her palm. She resisted the urge to slap him.

"You intrigued me from the first. I lingered in that inane class to see you." He pulled her closer now, "and you defied me - you resisted me."

He put a hand around her waist and his thumb stroked her back. "Aren't you curious? After all, *they* all must have found something they liked."

She pushed him now, shoving him away from her. He laughed.

"Not yet? Very well, I'll let the Vanto sully you first. I'm used to being asked to pick up the slack."

Eve turned to go and he quickly caught up, walking alongside. "I thought I was escorting you." He took her hand again, holding it out from himself. "I'll understand if you want to keep your distance. You might not trust yourself," he said almost too quietly for her to hear. He raised his voice a little. "I'm glad they told you good things."

"I don't know if I'd go that far. Some of them seemed quite threatening. They seem to think you'll be returning to them. May I suggest you do?"

"You may. I will kindly decline. I am too absorbed for them now."

"You will not have me. Not like that. I don't know why you pursue it."

"Perhaps I want more than that."

Eve stopped and looked at him. "I don't believe you."

"Oh, it's true. That's all I've wanted for some time now. But I saw part of you today, a part I desire as much as your smell and taste. A part you have already given that *Vanto*." He spat the word like a curse. He started walking again, and she moved with him, still confused.

When they reached the door, he turned her hand over and traced her fingertips.

"Charcoal," he murmured. "I would like to join you for lunch again tomorrow. Where would you be most comfortable?"

"I believe there is nowhere in this palace that I feel comfortable with you, but you may call on Mother and I here again. Good night, Louis."

He raised her stained fingers to his lips, "Good night, Eve."

*

"Adam," Bianca called to him through the door to Eve's room. "What is the matter, Adam?"

"It is not your concern, Mother," he called back.

"But you were in such high spirits earlier. What changed?"

He pulled the door open. His face was haggard, his eyes frenzied. "She isn't wearing my favour."

"Oh," Bianca murmured. "Well, I'm sure there is a reason. You probably distracted her with your entrance this evening. You certainly seemed to have turned her around. She was attentive, but downcast, all afternoon. Louis will do that to her, it seems. You had best finish him tomorrow," she threatened.

"Louis was here?" he asked as Eve came into the suite. She walked passed both of them without looking up.

"Eve?" Mother called. "May I come in?"

She was already pulling off her robe. "Yes, come in."

Adam instantly forgot his concern after seeing her. She was starting to remove her gown.

"Wait, Eve." He turned her gently, tears were already leaking from her eyes.

"I will not," she vowed. "I will not shed any more tears for that, that lout!"

"Eve?" Adam put his hand to her breast, where his pin had once resided.

"He broke it," she cried, throwing herself into his arms. "He took it and folded it. I don't even know where it is now. He just dropped it on the floor, like it was trash." She sobbed freely now and Adam stroked her hair.

"He did?" Bianca asked. She turned and left the room.

"I'm so glad I don't wear Lane's anymore." He could understand her concern. It was unlikely that one would be repaired.

"It's all right, Eve. I can repair it, or I can make another one. I was just worried there was another reason you weren't wearing it."

She backed up enough to look at him. "You didn't, you didn't think I..." she couldn't finish the thought. "No, Adam." She clutched him now. "Never."

"Here it is." Mother dropped the crumpled copper atop Jasper's paper bloom on the nightstand. "I'll let you two be. Sleep well. Everything will turn out for the best," she tried to assure them.

"This wasn't all, was it, Eve?" Adam asked, now pulling her onto the bed with him, cradling her in his lap.

"No. He – he kissed me again." She sniffled. "Said I should know what I was missing. And the women tonight... it was awful, Adam. The things they said. The things they implied." She put the heels of her hands to her eyes as though trying to press the images right out of her head.

"Martina had mentioned something about that last night. I would have never guessed. Why any woman... Don't think about that Eve. You are your own. You always will be. He can't have that."

"That was the last thing, the one that has me frightened. He said he wants a part of me that you already have. I don't know what he means, and I don't know how he means to get it."

"He wants it?" Adam snorted. Her ideas, her thoughts, anyone would want those. "Well I can't blame him for that. There isn't a man in the elite that wouldn't want it."

Eve flinched.

"Oh no, Eve." He laughed now. "There are a number of women in the elite who would want it, too. He saw your notebook today in the library. That's what he wants."

"Oh, well." She stood and took off her gown now. "He can't have that either." She smiled slyly.

Adam closed his eyes, not wanting to stare while she found her nightdress. He heard a creak just before her lips were at his ear.

"You can open them again," she teased.

He laughed again and grabbed for her, but she rolled away and under the covers.

CHAPTER NINE

Eve woke, as she had many mornings now, in Adam's arms. She continued to curl into him, waiting for him to stir. She wouldn't be able to wait much longer. With luck, she would spend part of the day with him.

"I hope Mother doesn't have anything important this afternoon. I really want to take you to the lab with me," he murmured as he awoke, tightening his hold.

"Yes! I want to be there. I'm sure Mother would excuse me for that." Eve had completely forgotten Adam's discovery in all of her distress the night before. She rolled over now and kissed him good morning. "I'm so glad I talked you into sharing the bed."

"I am too."

Eve spent the morning in a meeting with the High One and Vanto Ethan. There was a dispute between some of the Ducat that he wanted to advise the High One of before settling.

"Vanto," Mother asked as he finished, "what level of dishonour is it to destroy the favour of a vying suitor?"

Eve gasped a little. She hadn't even thought to report Louis' offence.

“Minor. Such scraps often result from two seeking the same hand. Usually a challenge is declared and accepted. The dispute eventually resolves itself.”

“Yes, thank you.” Mother did not look happy with this answer. Of course, in the past favours were never permanent. Stepping on an actual bloom would not incur the same wrath as the destruction of something crafted by hand.

Eve walked slowly back to the suite. She was dreading lunch. “Adam will be there,” Mother reminded her. Eve smiled and tried to step more lightly.

Adam was not in when they returned, but Louis was already seated at the table. Betty was standing next to the cart holding their lunches. Louis rose and bowed to the High One before taking Eve’s hand and kissing it. “Thank you again for allowing me to join you, Most High.”

She didn’t reply but moved to take a seat at the table. Louis moved to help with her chair. He took the opportunity to brush her cheek, as well.

Adam burst in moments later. “Nothing,” he grumbled. Then he looked up and saw the three at the table rather than two. “Excuse me, Most High.”

He stopped and straightened, standing next to Betty.

“Please, join us, Adam,” Eve said with a ready smile. Adam sat opposite Louis, each to one side of Eve. “Nothing?” she asked.

“I want to test the power, but I can’t find anything to test it with. I can feel the energy in the solution when I touch it.”

Eve gasped and grabbed at his hands to look at his fingers. Had he hurt himself?

“It’s not as powerful as that, Eve. It does tingle though,” he said with a smile.

“Power?” Louis asked now. He reached to take Eve’s other hand. She dropped Adam’s reluctantly to eat another bite.

"I would rather not discuss it until I have finished testing it, Highness," he told Louis coldly. "Mother, have you need of Eve this afternoon? I would appreciate her input into the experiment."

Eve noticed Mother looking at her over the table, no doubt judging how vital her afternoon attendance was. It would be better if Eve wasn't needed. She would have a hard time focusing until this situation was resolved.

"I had hoped to have her meet with Vinca Nancy, but yes, she should accompany you. If you have found a new power source, I would want the best minds working on it, and Eve is most definitely one of those."

Eve blushed. She was still unaccustomed to praise, especially from Mother. Louis smiled at her. She pretended not to notice.

"Well, as I have finished, perhaps I will go set things up in the lab," Adam excused himself.

"You know what this power source is, don't you, Eve?" Louis asked.

"Indeed. I am most curious myself. Why is Adam being so secretive?" Mother asked.

Eve licked her lips. Was it wrong of her to share his discovery? "It is an old source, re-discovered," she allowed, hoping they might solve it for themselves.

Mother's eye glittered. "Really?" She asked excitedly.

Eve smiled at Her and nodded. "We believe so. That's why we are testing today. If we are right..." She shook her head. The possibilities, as shown in the devices and relics left from long ago, were endless.

Louis still hadn't put it together for himself. His brow was furrowed. Eve smirked a little. He was not as bright as he liked to think.

"Well, I will keep his secret, but I demand to be among the first informed when it is confirmed!" The High One rose and strode from the room, leaving Eve alone with Louis, again.

"You cannot tell me more?" he pleaded with her, stroking her hand now.

"No," she said coolly.

"There is no way I might convince you?" he asked, turning her hand over and kissing her wrist. When she didn't answer, he placed another kiss on her elbow. He leaned toward her, his hand brushing her thigh.

She felt her stomach clench. "Stop!" she demanded.

"Is that really what you want?" he asked, turning his grey eyes up through curled lashes before running his nose along her upper arm. Her breath caught.

"Yes," she whispered through clenched teeth.

"Hmmm, that doesn't sound very definitive," he taunted and moved his lips to her shoulder, hovering just over the fabric of her dress. The table stopped him from moving all the way along her collarbone, but didn't stop him running his nose up her neck. She closed her eyes and began gasping, her skin tingling. This shouldn't feel good; it should revolt her.

"I did earn my reputation," he whispered in her ear, his hand moving on her leg again.

"Most High?" Betty interrupted. Louis shot her a glare, but Eve smiled broadly in thanks.

"Yes, Betty. I believe we are finished," she said, rising and shaking out her skirt. "I had best be in the lab. Adam will be waiting. Will you join me?" she asked Louis.

When he saw her hand held in his direction, he dropped his gaze from Betty and rose to take it. "The honour would be mine," he muttered.

"Thank you," Eve whispered to Betty, who winked as they passed.

Adam's eyes narrowed when he saw Louis on Eve's arm as she entered the lab. She quickly extracted herself though and half-ran to his bench. "This is it?" she asked, eyes wide.

Two metal pieces were clamped to the edge of the beaker, half submerged. A copper wire ran between them. “What metals are you using?” she asked.

“Silver and copper.”

“Why is it green?” She examined the copper strip.

“It seems to be reacting with the solution.”

Eve clapped her hands. “This is marvelous!”

“I see no power,” Louis complained.

Adam pulled a pair of metal snips and clipped the wire, shaking his hand slightly as he did so. “It runs through the wire,” he explained.

Eve reached out before Louis had the chance. She closed her fingers around the opening in the wire and felt the sting as the power jumped through her before continuing its circuit. She squealed with glee and threw her arms around Adam. She dropped them just as quickly. This was too public a place for such a display.

Louis took his turn now. He didn’t flinch, but narrowed his eyes. “The power of light?” he asked, looking at the pair of them.

Eve smiled broadly and bounced on her toes.

Adam’s grin was smug. “Yes. Eve gave me the clues.”

“Well, this is hardly conclusive evidence, being subjective,” he argued. He moved to another bench and pulled out a metal flake. Eve shot a look of question at Adam, but he simply shrugged. She followed Louis to his bench now.

He held the silvery fragment between two pairs of tongs and was heating it in the fire. It began to glow quickly. He pulled either end with the tongs and stretched it, creating a thin wire. The centre began to sag. He spun one hand in a circle while lifting the wire from the fire. As it cooled, the coil he had made froze in place.

“And what is that?” she asked him.

“A new metal. I extracted it from that ore.” He nodded toward the lumps on his desk. “I found it very easy to work with once heated, although it breaks easily. It doesn’t melt, but it does glow with a moderate amount of heat." Eve had just seen this for herself. He tipped the thread toward her. "Gentle, it is fragile," he warned.

Eve took hold of either end of the metal just above the tongs and Louis released it. Together, they walked back to Adam's bench. Eve held her breath and touched each end to the broken copper wire. The metal coil lit up.

She set the wire down gently in front of the beaker before joining in the laughter and applause around them. She threw her arms around Louis now and kissed his cheek. "Wonderful!" she cried. She turned and hugged Adam again. "Amazing!"

She was still jumping up and down as the men glared at each other.

"Enough!" she told them both. "You each had a hand in this. You," she took Adam's hand, "discovered the method. And you," she took Louis' hand, "built the proof. Now, be happy! We have the power of light!" She started dancing around the lab in glee.

She grabbed Ernst Derek by the shoulders and began swinging him around with her. He was grinning madly, as well. He grabbed her by the waist and swung her. Then Derek found a Ducati who had stopped what she was doing and was still staring awestruck at the bench. He picked her up and spun her, too. Eve linked elbows with another Prince and danced him around as well.

She came back to bench and pinched both men on the leg. "I said enough." She left them again to dance once more.

*

"Metals," Adam muttered.

"Yes. I have a way with them. You may have noticed." Louis looked to Eve's hand which was once more on Derek as they danced around the room.

"Indeed." Adam followed his gaze and finally shook his head. Now that his eyes were no longer on Louis, he couldn't deny the beauty and glee that was being spread from Eve throughout the lab. More and more people were giving over and dropping their careful non-contact to kiss cheeks, hug one another, and dance freely. “She’s going to change the world, you know that,” he murmured to no one in particular.

“She seems well on her way,” Louis answered.

Eve grabbed Adam’s hand and swung him into the arms of one of the Ducati. Then she linked Louis’ arm and circled between him and Derek.

Eventually, the display became too much. The sound of black powder brought Eve out of her happy trance.

“Who did that?!” she yelled.

One Prince stepped out from a bench, blushing. Eve shook her head.

Just then, the post noon bell rang. Everyone poured out the door together. They would be late for dinner.

Louis pecked her cheek as he ran past. “I’ll win you tonight,” he assured her, his tone jovial.

Adam put an arm around her waist. “I think not,” he said with a smile of his own. She would be his forever.

“I’m glad you two stopped going for one another’s throat, if only for a short time. This is a day of celebration. We must tell Mother.”

Adam couldn’t quite understand why she continued to use the honour form, but he picked her up by the waist and ran for the suite holding her in front of him. She laughed madly.

“What is all the ruckus?” Mother asked as they burst through the door.

“The power of light, of course,” Eve said, twirling once and then planting a kiss on Adam’s lips. “Was the yellow gown cleaned, Betty? I want to wear it again tonight,” she said as she headed for the room.

“You’ve proven it?” Bianca asked her son.

“I had help,” he admitted reluctantly.

“Of course you did,” his mother looked to the door of Eve’s room.

"Sadly, not only hers. Louis produced a metal that glows with the power."

"Well! That is still wonderful news. Will you share it in the hall tonight?" she asked.

"I think I must. Everyone in the lab today will be spreading the word. She is amazing, Mother. She had all of them dancing. I've never seen so much touching in one room before! Derek must have kissed every cheek there, even mine!"

Mother laughed. "Oh I do wish I'd been there to see that. Maybe she will create as much of a stir in the hall tonight."

"I doubt that. There were mostly young people in the lab. I can't see... Prince Grant for instance, picking up and whirling a girl he isn't related to." Grant was about as stuffy as the elder Princes came.

Bianca laughed aloud again. "No, no. I suppose not. Well, I'm going to change into something more festive myself."

Adam entered Eve's room and found her in the yellow gown looking for a different robe. "Green?" she asked, pulling out a deeply dyed one.

"That looks lovely," he said, removing his shirt. "What power do you possess?" he asked, wrapping his arms around her again. "Can we bottle that and spread it through the elite? I think we could use some of it." He kissed her.

"I have no power, just an abundance of enthusiasm." She buried her nose in his chest, and he laughed.

"Well, that has certainly started to spread." He pulled out a new shirt and jacket.

"Indeed."

Louis was waiting outside the suite again. His smile seemed more genuine now. Eve was happy to return it.

"May I escort you, Eve?"

"You may." She extended a hand. "Thank you for your help in the lab."

"You don't need to thank me," he said. "It was a pleasure to please you."

Her face fell a little.

"No. I meant... it was worth it to see you so happy."

Her smile came back though a little smaller than before. "Have you named your new metal?" she asked.

"I was thinking Evenite," he said.

"I am easily broken, but light up brightly?" she laughed.

Adam was almost snarling. Bianca patted his hand. "Down. She's happy; let her be happy," she whispered to him.

"Something like that," Louis said with a chuckle of his own. "That colour looks amazing on you. I think I told you so last night."

"Yes? It is in honour of the power of light. Adam chose it," she said, looking over her shoulder with a broad smile for him.

Adam smirked. He was in her bedroom; she had just said so. Louis' smile slipped and his lip curled back.

*

As they entered the hall and passed the Cargon table, Eve's smile fell away entirely. How had she forgotten the match? How had she forgotten what was at stake? How had she forgotten his treatment at lunch? Eve pulled her hand away just before they reached the High Table. She sat and put a hand to her head.

"Eve?" Mother asked as she sat beside Her. "Are you well?"

"I think so. Just getting a little spun around these days. Highs and lows in rapid succession."

"Do you want to talk about it?"

Eve sat back as the first course was placed in front of her. "All right..." She took a sip of wine. "Louis pressed further... than I would have liked, after you left."

Mother's eyes blazed. "He did," she said coldly.

"Betty was wonderful. She brought me to my senses, and we left for the lab." She shook her head, remembering. "I was so happy there. I could have kissed my worst enemy in that lab today." She grinned. "It was amazing!" She sat back with a sigh. "And now I'm reminded that my fate rests on that board. Just as it always has." Eve closed her eyes.

Mother patted her arm. "Your fate is your own. Your hand rests on that board, that alone. If Louis presses you again, you simply report him and he will be properly lowered. He may not face punishment for ruining Adam's favour, but forcing himself on a woman is definitely a high crime."

"He didn't go that far," Eve admitted, her eyes shifting.

"Did you ask him to stop?"

"I did."

"Then he was in the wrong. Don't stand for it," Mother warned. "We have a society that respects one's person."

"Yes, Mother," Eve agreed, blushing. "I pray Adam wins, and I need never be in the situation ever again."

"I'm sure he will, dear. I'm sure he will," Bianca said with a smile.

Adam rose before dessert was served. "Prince Louis, do you wish to share the news or shall I?" he asked across the hall.

"Vanto," Louis said, bowing to him.

"We have made a discovery today that I'm sure many of you have heard about by now. With the help of Prince Louis, I was able to prove a source of the power of light in a saline solution."

There were murmurs throughout the hall. "And now, I shall leave you to your meal," he said and walked to the Cargon table. Louis rose again and joined him.

Tonight, Eve did not rise when the men resumed their game. She put a finger to her mouth, biting a nail. She hadn't talked to Adam about his strategy. He didn't need her help, she reminded herself. She finished another glass of wine and watched as more and more people left.

Some of Louis' admirers approached her, but she raised a hand to dismiss them; she couldn't deal with that tonight. She kept her eyes on the board, it was nearing an end. It was still either player's Game.

Mother rose and joined Adam. Eve motioned for another glass of wine. "Most High?" Eve turned and saw Lane filling her cup.

She took a deep breath. "I'm scared," she told him honestly. "I'm scared of the outcome."

He filled her cup. "You have friends; they are always here for you."

She nodded, smiling toward him. "Thank you," she whispered.

He bowed and backed away.

Eve drank her third glass of wine as her nerves continued to get the better of her. When the cup was empty, she stood slowly, knowing her feet were likely to be unsteady. She walked carefully toward the Cargon table. The room swayed as she walked and she knew she was veering ever so slightly to the right. She stopped at the edge of the table.

Eve tried to watch the game, but it seemed the pieces kept moving on their own. She would see an open path and then wonder when neither player took it. She would watch a move she was sure was illegal, but then the pieces shifted in her vision such that it wasn't. She had no idea who was winning or how much longer the game would last.

*

Adam watched Eve's approach. How much wine had she drunk? She was swaying dangerously. He worried she might fall. She made it to the table, however, and clung to its wooden edge. He turned his attention back to the Game.

Bianca came to Eve's side. "Fool, girl," she gently reprimanded. "Of all the nights to drink your fill. Well, I suppose this way you won't remember the good or the bad ending." She put an arm around Eve's shoulders and helped her stand upright.

Louis smiled toward Eve and made another move on board. Adam frowned, taking time in his next placement. He watched Louis eyeing Eve again. His smile was no longer laughing, it was leering. He was thinking something hideous, Adam was certain. He looked to Eve again himself. She was flushed, a sheen of perspiration on her brow; her scent was stronger for it. He pressed his lips in a line, no wonder Louis was staring. He set his jaw and moved again.

Adam saw the end. He saw a line of moves that could not be thwarted. He counted. Even or odd? Even. He moved, knowing, as Jasper had, that he was beaten. He could only pray Louis made a mistake.

Louis looked to Eve again before moving. He smiled broadly at her then moved confidently.

Adam moved once more in defeat. Unless Louis erred in his next move, the game was over.

Eve suddenly collapsed under the table. Louis moved quickly and then dashed to her side. Adam turned and left the room.

*

Eve's eyes fluttered open. She was in the hall, looking at the ceiling; it needed dusting. She saw Mother's face out of the corner of her eye and Lane on the other side. Was this a chance to make another choice? Then Lane stepped back and the choice was gone.

"I am sorry, Mother." Eve struggled to sit. "I let my nerves get the better of me." She groaned as the room spun around her.

"Finished, Most High," Louis declared, setting his hand behind Eve. "Eve? Are you all right?" he asked.

"I had too much wine," she admitted.

He sighed. "Is that all it was?" He put his lips to her forehead, and it was surprisingly tender. "I am glad you are well."

"I don't know if I'd go that far," she murmured, trying to put her feet beneath her. Louis held her hand and waist to help her up. She leaned heavily on his arm until she could shift her weight to the table. She saw Mother tending the board. The Game was over. She looked to Louis.

"You?" she asked. He grinned and nodded. She nodded, too. "Please help me to my room?" she asked. "Husband."

His grin broadened and he put a hand to her waist, guiding her step.

At the door to her suite, Eve turned. "Thank you, Louis. I am sure we can deal with any formalities in the days to come. I will see you tomorrow." She opened the door behind her. He continued to hold her hand.

"Should I not help you to your room?" he asked from the door.

Adam opened the bedroom door and glared. He came to Eve's side. "I will help her, Highness. Good night."

"Good night, Vanto." Louis turned.

"Silly, Eve," Adam murmured. He put an arm under her knees and lifted her into his arms. "Silly, silly girl." He kissed her warm, flushed cheek. She sighed.

"I am going to wake from this dream, aren't I?" she asked.

"I'm afraid not," he said in a quiet sad voice.

She sat up more and looked into his eyes. "I fell asleep in the library. One of the Librarians is going to come and wake me. I will be removed from service. All a dream," she mumbled, her eyes drifting shut.

*

Adam clenched his jaw, fighting tears. How had he lost? How?

Mother came behind him. "Is she asleep?"

"Yes, she's dreaming." His voice was breaking.

"You sleep, too. We'll work through this. What you have is strong enough to endure it. I already told you that." She kissed her son's cheek and left him to carry Eve to her bed.

He slowly pulled off her clothing. She was so fragile, so precious. He pulled back the covers and shifted her to the sheets. He moved to the far side.

"Adam?" she called after he'd turned down the last lantern.

"Yes, Eve?"

"Who am I?"

"Eve," he said, a little exasperated. Of all the nights to drink too much.

"Show me who I am?" she asked. She rolled toward him and put her body against his. "Remind me who I am?" She kissed his jaw, his ear, his neck. "Who am I?" she asked one last time.

He couldn't answer; she was everything. Instead, he gave in and pulled her closer, kissing her with abandon. He would not lose her tonight.

*

Eve sat her horse, back straight. She would not cry. "Goodbye, Mother. Goodbye, brother," she said and blew a kiss to both of them. "Louis?" she asked, turning to face him.

"Yes." He turned his horse and she wheeled hers to follow. She blew Adam one last kiss over her shoulder.

She did not know what she would find in Augustia. She did not know how she would survive the day without Adam at the end of it. She took one more deep breath. She would be a credit to her duty.

"Eve? Is everything all right?" Louis asked her.

"Yes. I told you, I've never left the palace." She was glad to have such an acceptable reason for fear and trepidation. She did not need to admit to the others.

"Right. It has been a long time since I left last. We'll watch out for each other," he suggested.

Eve nodded.

*

Adam watched her go. He was empty. He was alone. He was nothing. He had no purpose, no goal, no worth. When she was here, he could convince himself he was furthering her ideas, meeting her needs. Without her....

"Come, Adam." When he didn't move, Bianca returned to the palace without him.

ABOUT THE AUTHOR

Mother and wife, Kimberly divides her time between family, part-time job as an environmental consultant and pursuit of her imagination. Summers are her field season, spent working hard outdoors, but travel time and winter are when she expresses the daydreams explored in those long days.

Visit her Web site at www.kimmydonn.com

MARTIN SISTERS PUBLISHING

WWW.MARTINSISTERSPUBLISHING.COM

8872402R0

Made in the USA
Charleston, SC
22 July 2011